UNCLE

By Julia Markus

NOVELS

Uncle, A Houghton Mifflin Award Novel
American Rose
Friends Along the Way
A Change of Luck
Patron of the Arts (a novella)

BIOGRAPHIES

Dared and Done. The Marriage of Elizabeth Barrett and Robert Browning
Across An Untried Sea. Discovering Lives Hidden
in the Shadow of Convention and Time
J. Anthony Froude. The Last Undiscovered Great Victorian

Uncle

Julia Markus

Print ISBN-13: 978–1977543462
Ebook ASIN: B072QZ4DX6

For Marjorie

PART ONE

One Spring Day Irv Bender gave up his chances in life for his younger brother. Irv was sixteen. He was standing at the top of the concrete staircase outside of Snyder High School. He made his decision from that height, looking down on the Boulevard and the monotonous rows of one-family houses across the street. On that spring day in Jersey City the sun had dissolved the clouds, and the remote sky appeared to be the color of aquamarine. The dust in the air was stirred by the breeze and the smell of something sweet could be discerned through the must. Irv had his revelation. Fat, awkward, adolescent, he stood firmly at the height, while his spirit swooned and he gave himself away.

He walked home alone to Stegman Parkway. His mother's flat was the first floor of a house. It had a screened-in front porch. His mother was sitting out. She wore a dark, patterned cotton house-dress. When she looked up at him her eyes said, "Well?" That's what they always said. Perhaps she had been waiting for this moment.

He told her he was quitting school. He would get a job. She tried to dissuade him — out of guilt? out of convention? He never knew. Years later, late at night, someone suggested she might have meant her words. But Irv knew better. All of her concern was for his brother. When she looked at Babe her eyes said, "Whatever, forever."

Mother and older son became accomplices. They sacrificed him for his brother.

Irv's mother and father were East European Jews. America had not done much for them. Irv's father drank and gambled and

1

died. The mother got along; she got along. Education *was* life to his mother. It was the form of discipline and self-denial that paid off. To wish Babe an education was to wish him everything good.

What did she know? In her ignorance she had more excuse than most for favoring the beautiful and the quick. Babe was the brilliant one, he'd go far.

But as it happened, Babe stopped short, while Irv worked out his destiny.

He began at sixteen, exhilarated by his decision. His brother, in effect, was his first love — the first love of a sensitive boy, a boy who was able to give himself away.

Really, it was Irv who should have gone on in school. Babe a doctor? Impossible. He hadn't the brains. Irv had brains. Directed into channels, he might have become a professor of something — philosophy? art? He wouldn't have become a doctor-doctor either.

But what might have been is never exposed to chance, only to logic. Irv went into the world unchanneled, alone, without one thought for himself. He lost his self for his brother.

He started from exactly where he was. He got a job at the Jewish Y on Bergen Avenue. General work. His father had been pretty well known there. He had always spent a part of each day in the steam. The rich men took to Solly's son. He was thorough, quiet, unattached. One thing led to another. Irv had eyes to see.

By the time Irv was twenty-one he had bought the house on Stegman Parkway for his mother, and Babe was in his first year at NYU.

Then the crash came. It didn't hurt Irv. He was a rumrunner. He stood on a boat in the dark while the liquor was unloaded. He held a gun he couldn't shoot.

When Prohibition ended, he was with the men who went legit. He was offered a good job in an import liquor firm. He persuaded the men to hire his brother instead.

That Babe graduated NYU at all was a testament to the will of their mother. Clearly, he could go no further. Irv was there when Babe told the mother the truth. A queer sensuous expression crossed her face: "You see, from you I can take this." She did not cry. Babe was flushed with gratitude. He was a coward and had expected worse.

"Don't worry, Babe," Irv said. "I'll find something good for you." His mother looked at Irv skeptically, "Well?"

There was room in the import firm for a college graduate; Babe took the job Irv could have had.

Irv could have worked Babe in some other way. This was his first selfish act. Perhaps he was punishing his brother for having let the family down, sending him off to work like that. Still, Irv needed time off.

All the time he had worked illegally he had felt glorious — like a woman who would stop at nothing for her lover or her son. But now, some instinct kept him from becoming a liquor salesman. At twenty-five he had an intimation of his worth.

Often he'd go to Greenspan's for lunch. He'd walk all the way from Stegman Parkway to the Square, thinking, wondering. He liked Greenspan's. All the young lawyers just graduated and out of work would sit around talking. Greenspan's was the place for conversation.

Interesting stuff. Intelligent men, young, thin, intense, with ideas about what people needed. Irv was a good listener. Sometimes he treated for soup. Not often. He was no sop.

One day he was sitting alone, reading a paper and keeping an ear to the conversation behind him. Norman Thomas had been driven out of Jersey City the night before, sent through the turnstile, then pushed onto the Tube back to New York. The men behind Irv were incensed. Anything might happen in retaliation.

A man walked over to him. "Hi, Irv. Long time. Can I join you?"
"Sure."

Irv hadn't talked with Mandy Mershheimer since high school. They had played basketball together. Basketball was the only sport Irv played well. When he took the job at the Y he always loved to hear the sound of a basketball passed down along the court. Sometimes, at first, he'd get into a game.

He had seen Mandy a few times in Greenspan's. They had nodded. Mandy worked for the *Jersey Journal*. He had been waiting for the right time to approach Irv.

Mandy had an imagination. Therefore he was curious about fat, silent Irv, always dressed meticulously in a dark suit, his narrow eyes always hidden by shades. It was said Irv Bender was a tough man and that if you crossed him you were dead. Mandy thought he might be worth a story. Not one of the stories he wrote for the *Jersey Journal*, but one of those he wrote when he sat at his desk pretending to write for the *Jersey Journal*.

Irv realized at once that Mandy was interested in him. A man's enthusiasm was an entirely new experience for Irv. He was flattered and in response grew more silent.

So Mandy talked. He was a good talker. But so young. He believed if one person didn't talk the other had to. He believed his enthusiasm was the common lot, so he had no sense of responsibility about its effect on others.

He had to do so much talking to fill the empty space that soon he was talking about himself. And, eureka, he cracked Irv.

"You write stories?" Irv repeated.

"That's the sad truth."

"About what?" Irv asked.

"About life, about people, about the heart. No one publishes them."

Irv smiled; he was enchanted. "I always knew there was more!" he said to Mandy. "Go on. Don't be discouraged. You'll be published some day."

That day when Mandy got home he found a letter accepting a story. The next day he treated Irv to lunch.

"It had nothing to do with *me*."

"That's okay," Mandy said, waving his hand magnanimously. "Still, I want to treat."

"You writers are very superstitious."

"With a good-luck charm like you, why not?"

They had lunch together every day. Irv's mother wouldn't dare express it, but Irv knew what she was saying: "You'll end up like your father yet!"

Not true. Irv was in a tumult of expectation. There was more.

There was, for example, the imagination. Irv hadn't one. He had intelligence and he had an eye. He saw. But he did not alter what he saw. He had excellent business sense.

Baby-faced Mandy — kinky, sandy hair, big dark eyes, puffy lips that shivered around words — didn't have much business acumen. Many many years later, when his face had weathered and he had learned when not to speak, he signed a contract for a fabulous sum. "Who ever taught you about business?" his new agent joked.

He was very serious for a moment: "Irving Bender."

But back in the days when Mandy had only sold one story, if he had a dime he spent it, if he had a dollar it went.

Irv noticed. He thought it the Achilles' heel of the imaginative. "You should be more careful."

"Why?" asked Mandy. "If this number comes out (he had just boxed 713 before getting on with his lunch), I'll be able to buy my camp without my father's help."

"Your camp?"

"Sure," said Mandy, as if Irv knew all about it.

They began to take trips in Mandy's car. Irv sat beside him looking out the window, seeing the country scenes pass by. A most reflective time.

When Mandy came to Stegman Parkway to pick Irv up, Irv's mother never said, "Have a good trip." She said, "Summer camps? Go know."

Irv thought about this in the car. His mother had no idea. But was she right? Was it crazy? What did she know?

He looked at Mandy humming away, daydreaming. What did *he* know?

One day Mandy let Irv drive. Irv drove very well. He kept his eyes on the road and went fast. He made his decision. He trusted himself.

Late that fall they found the camp they wanted. They stood on the hill. The clear cold air budged the big clouds. The cold blue sky shone. Mandy's cheeks were red. He danced. To the left hop, shuffle, hop back. To the right hop, shuffle, hop back. Irv adjusted his shades.

The agent said, "Your friend seems satisfied."

Irv said, "He's easily pleased."

By the time that very spot in Pennsylvania was covered with snow, Irv had completed the negotiations. He had simply shut up and waited. He had the talent of looking straight into a man's eyes and saying nothing. In those days he needed shades for courage. And he had so little money left that he had to make the best deal. He owed it to his family to drive a man down, to see revealed in a man's eyes the very skeleton of his expectations.

As he grew older he didn't have to rely on his shades; he could stare baldly until he saw the sparse dance of death in the other man's eyes.

Still, Irv invested everything he had in the camp — a third of what Mandy raised. Mandy said they were equal partners anyway. Things divide easily by two. Mandy said no written contract. Word of mouth. Partners. Brothers. Friends.

"Okay," said Irv, after a pause.

Mandy made lists of names for the camp. He was engrossed in the work:

Adam and Eve
Aladdin
Atlantis
Aurora

were some of the A's.

Irv read through the alphabet. "What about Camp Long Lake?"

Mandy groaned. "A rose by any other name ..."

"Rose Lake," said Irv.

It was settled.

"And what will I do with this list now?" Mandy sighed, pointing to his notebook.

"Publish it."

One had imagination, rich relatives, connections. The other had good eyes and a good head. One dreamed of making enough money in the summer to be able to write all winter long. The other wanted to make money and was willing to work every day of the year — but not as a liquor salesman. No, that wouldn't have come from his own skin. He wanted to build something from his own skin.

Babe didn't want to be a liquor salesman, either. Irv had trouble persuading people to switch him into the office; they wanted to let him go.

One night Irv's mother waited up for him. "What's wrong?" he asked.

"Babe's thinking of getting married."

"Who to?" He sat down.

"Milton Schwartz's daughter, Esther. A nice girl," she said as if she were practicing.

Mother and son looked at each other. They did not speak.

Irv went to Babe's room. Babe was sitting on the windowsill, looking out, smoking.

"Can't sleep?"

Babe put his head back and closed his eyes. In the dim light his face was hollows and shadows. Then he opened his eyes. He looked stunned. Every time he had a problem he looked at his brother like that — as if he saw enough to confuse him, or nothing at all.

"Ma tell you?"

"Yes."

Babe smiled very enigmatically.

Esther came to the house. She seemed sturdily built around a principle of propriety. She said, "Benjamin said this, Benjamin said that. Mrs. Bender, I want to tell you what Benjamin said."

Benjamin?

Underneath her statuesque control, something was steaming. She'd look at Babe, and Irv felt something strange and wild going on in her. Then she'd Benjamin-this-and-that until it passed.

Babe looked all dressed up like a Christian on Sunday.

Something was crazy. Irv talked to Mandy. They had been together signing up campers and stopped at the Square for Danish and coffee.

"I don't know what's happening to my brother. He's disappearing in front of my eyes."

"Is he going to bed with her?"

"That's between them," Irv answered, but he felt sick.

"Is it ever!"

"All I know is something's wrong. When the two of them are together, there's no air to breathe."

"You'll get used to that," said Mandy knowingly. But he knew no more than Irv of the woe that can lead to marriage.

Actually, he knew *less* than Irv, who said, "It's as if he's afraid of being Babe. He wants suddenly to become 'Benjamin.'" He imitated Esther.

"His prerogative to grow up, no?"

"Is that the way you grow up, Mandy? You go out and find someone who'll call you Benjamin?"

"Well, your brother's known for his shortcuts."

The next week his mother said to Irv, sadly — it was very hard for her to lose Babe — "I think Babe wants to buy Esther a ring."

Irv said, "It's no good."

"Mr. Expert!" she said, ridiculing him. "What do you know about what a man and a woman feel for each other?" The words came from her heart.

He thought he would die. Misfits *should* die. Then his hatred turned. He used his bulk as a bulwark. He was as far from her as his body would allow.

"How much?"

"She's a nice girl. We shouldn't look mean. It wouldn't be right."

"Just let me know the price."

Irv threw himself into the camp. At his center he was clear as ice. But the center was surrounded by a fog in which he was lost. For he could not help his brother, whom he loved more than life.

From the time he was a small boy, it was always Babe who let the door bang and dragged things in. Things full of dirt or brightly colored things. Babe was indiscriminate and life was wonderful. Mrs. Bender, can Babe come out to play? He brought little kids in. When Babe was little the apartment was full of kids. Babe was remarkable, absolutely remarkable, Irv had always thought.

Now he was older and he brought home Esther Schwartz. But without joy and without marveling at the abundance of the earth. He had stayed outside too long. It had gotten dark. He was scared.

Irv wanted to hold him in his arms, protect him, tell him not to be afraid. But what did he know? Years later, in a church he had to go into, he saw an altar painting of a Virgin Mary with her red heart torn right out of her chest, fully exposed. He remembered the time Babe was engaged to Esther and he felt for a moment the old gash of vulnerability.

One night Babe came into Greenspan's. Irv and Mandy were eating pecan Danish while Mandy explained the meaning of the term "dénouement." He had used it in a story — satirically. Irv now read all of Mandy's stories. They were remarkable, simply remarkable. Mandy went outside and described everything the way it never happened at all. Or the way it could have or should have or almost happened. Irv was beginning to catch on.

"Hey," Mandy said with his mouth full, "here comes Benjamin."

Babe came over and sat down. Later, when Mandy described Babe, he described only his dark blue eyes, slightly wet, slightly absent, overgrown. Babe looked over the table: pecan Danish crumbs, coffee cups, an ashtray filled with butts, Mandy's long lean hands, Irv's blunt fat fingers. Babe's eyes said, "So what? There'll be a million tables like this in life and I won't be served at any of them."

Mandy flicked an ash. Bedroom eyes. Sad, sexy Babe, mama's pride and joy. Babe looked at his brother. Mandy couldn't draw the line between self-pity and desperation. "See me?" Babe's eyes cried out. "I'm Exhibit A. One of the crumbs on the table."

"Anything wrong, Babe?" Mandy asked.

"Anything right?" Babe answered.

"Hell, you've got your whole life ahead of you," Mandy said.

Babe smiled ironically and looked over the table. "You're a dreamer, Mandy, so you got dreams ahead of you."

"And me?" Irv asked. "What do I got that makes me better off than you?"

"*Besides* from mama and me? Brother dear, you got brains."

"So do you."

Babe looked at Irv. "But you know how to use them. Do you realize there's a whole world out there," he motioned lazily past Greenspan's front door, "that's got arms and legs and hearts and brains all jumbled up? It's a St. Vitus's dance going on out there, everyone shaking away, trying to jiggle all the parts in place."

"That's quite an image," Mandy said. "Why don't you write it down?"

"Where's the part that holds the pen?" Babe asked.

Mandy shrugged. "This is some kid brother," he said to Irv.

"Exceptional," Irv said.

"Yeah," said Babe. "They should have sent me to the A. Harry Moore School for Exceptional Children." He gave a little spastic quirk.

"They may yet," Mandy said. But he had been touched and upset. At the same time, the artist in him became excited. "I don't get it," continued Mandy, the future master of the rewrite. "If things are really bothering you, can't you change them?"

Babe's eyes lit up for a moment. He had his brother's love of words that walked the edge. "Change them for what?"

Mandy was at a loss. He himself changed them for what he could get down on paper.

"Change them into whatever you want," Irv said. He gave the kid too much rope.

"What do I want, Irv?"

Irv said very slowly, "Maybe you want to get out of this engagement?"

"And change it for another?" Babe replied.

"Change it for nothing! Where's there the law you got to get married?"

"One thing leads to another," Babe said.

"You got to get married?" asked Mandy.

"Hey, don't start! I'm engaged to a girl who's worth ten of me!" Babe turned to Irv and asked, "Do you like Esther?"

"I don't know her."

"I want you to like her."

When Babe spoke of Esther he spoke with a mixture of shame and pride. For he believed he was sneaking past himself onto the road of righteousness.

"Why so silent, brother?" Babe asked. "You know you scare Esther by being so silent? She doesn't have much confidence in herself. She thinks you don't like her."

"What's there not to like?"

"See, I told her she was wrong about you," Babe said. Ironically? Hard to tell. He always spoke into a world of spite.

"So she's what you want," Irv said. "And a home and a family. What could be wrong with that?"

"You say it like it's something strange," Babe said, but he was frightened.

"For me it would be."

"Me too," said Mandy. "When I settle down, it'll be with a good typist or not at all."

Babe looked at them. Esther said she felt sorry for the two of them, they were loners and life got lonelier as you got older. And Babe, getting a grip on his new self turned his self-pity outward. "Irv, don't you want a wife someday? The world goes round two by two."

"Like mama and papa," Irv said, "the world goes round and round and round."

"But that's the way things are!" Babe said desperately. "You can't change the world."

"We sent you to school! You could have changed the world!"

"Me?" Babe said. "ME? You should have saved your money. I'm nothing! Nothing! Nothing!" He shook. His eyes filled with tears.

"Okay, kid, okay. Calm down," Mandy said, not knowing what to do.

"He's excitable," Irv explained.

"Another nervous bridegroom," Mandy tried, but he turned away.

"I'm all right, I'm all right. I'm very tired, that's all."

Irv was pale. He sat there like a stone while his brother cried out in pain.

Babe looked over the table once more. "I guess I'll get going."

"I'll come with you," Irv said.

"No. Please. I'll see you later." He got up and left.

"I shouldn't have said that about school."

"Ah, why not? That's not what's bothering him."

"Then what is?"

Mandy shrugged and said what he thought of Babe's eyes. Irv said Esther was the wrong woman. The two of them sat in Greenspan's and talked the night away. Babe stayed out. Walking. Walking. Getting nowhere.

Babe and Esther were married in the new temple on the Boulevard. Irv had never been in it. It reminded him of the new Loew's theatre with its swoop of space and colored glass. The rabbi spoke like an English actor. He formed each word lovingly and slid it out of his mouth moist and whole.

Babe was ethereal in his dark blue suit, which emphasized his pale skin and wild blue eyes. His hand was shaky when Irv passed him the ring.

Esther looked starched under her white gown. She stood in front of the tabernacle wholly convinced.

When it was all over, Babe raised his foot the way he used to when he was in a tantrum and with one stamp smashed the glass to smithereens. It made a loud noise — a sigh of release.

Afterward, Irv stood by himself for a moment at the top of the temple's stairs. He looked down at the Boulevard. It was late October and a clean cold breeze had cleared the air. He could smell leaves burning. He had spent most of the month at the camp, but even here in Jersey City there was a sense of harvest. It was over. He tasted peace.

Babe came to him. "How do you like this, brother? I'm a married man." He was tremendously relieved. He had signed a contract, worked himself into the pattern of men.

"I'm happy for you," Irv said, in the voice of a man who has not been happy and has had a presentiment that he won't be. His voice was tough, competent. He would watch the ways of the world.

Babe stood there flushed and wild and overdressed in the morning light. "You've been wonderful to me, brother. I love you." He rushed into Irv's arms with all the old verve of his outdoor life come back. And savage love ripped the peace out of Irv's heart as he felt his brother warm, vulnerable, happy in his arms.

In those years before the war Camp Rose Lake did not make money. Mandy could not quit his job. Irv sold real estate on the side. Yet the camp was growing in reputation. Mandy attracted. Irv watched Mandy in people's homes. He was charming, lovable. He seemed always to be saying, if you like me, I'll like you. A pact. Once people liked him, he was home. Then Irv explained the contract.

"Are there toilets in the bunkhouses?"

"No."

Mandy always wanted to say, "Not yet." But here Irv kept him down. Irv could say no unequivocally and he wouldn't let Mandy mitigate for a smile.

"But they have them at Badger Village."

Irv would shrug and look straight into mama or papa's eyes. Mandy squirmed in the silence.

"The food's kosher?"

Imperially, Irv allowed, "Nothing but the best."

The big young man sat straight in his chair and when he spoke his mouth moved sparingly. He loomed — a presence. Even without his shades his face was mask-like. The skin tight, pressing down the small nose, narrowing the eyes.

"Yes, we've heard from the Feins that the food is very good," mama or papa admitted.

"Them you trust?" Irv said with a slight grin. Seeing him smile, most people laughed aloud.

Then the war broke out. One day Irv was sitting on his porch at Stegman Parkway doing accounts when Mandy drove up and walked to the stoop in a navy uniform.

Irv looked at Mandy. He looked and looked and looked till he saw what Mandy had done.

"Well?" Mandy asked, stretching his hands out into the position of "nu?" His face was flushed and abandoned. He presented himself proudly to his friend.

What could Irv say? Irv did not yet know that if you live long enough you see everything. Mandy stood guileless in his bell-bottom trousers smiling, waiting, while Irv kept staring at an aberration.

"You've enlisted." Irv still did not believe it. He held the camp accounts in his hand.

Mandy stood still, his hands cupped upward, waiting for a downpour of affection.

"What about Rose Lake?" Irv asked.

Mandy's posture collapsed. "This is *war*, God damn it! War!" he yelled.

"You should have told me."

"I *am* telling you."

"You couldn't wait to be drafted?"

Of course he couldn't. He was following his destiny. And in front of his vision of the future, the past failed and fell away. Irv looked at a new man.

"You of all people!" Mandy said. "I thought you'd understand. Damn it, I thought you *knew*."

"I'll never understand," Irv said slowly.

"Betrayer!" their hearts cried out to each other.

Mandy looked abused.

Irv looked furious.

"Blind fool!" they thought of each other.

Mandy looked past the porch.

Irv looked at Mandy.

"What are you, a stone wall?" Mandy shouted finally, when Irv did not speak.

Irv *could not* speak. He stood up instead, turned his back and left Mandy alone on the porch.

Mandy noticed that Irv didn't take the accounts he had been working on. In an act of attrition he put an ashtray on the papers so they would not blow away.

Once Irv had slept and woken and slept and woken again, his world came back to him. He made his peace with Mandy. After all, he should have known better than to have trusted him. Who was he? Someone who walked into Greenspan's and sat down.

Partner?

Still.

Friend?

All right.

But no brother.

❧ ❧ ❧

Babe was drafted toward the end of the war.

He lived in the upstairs apartment with Esther and his daughter, Suzanne. Nine months and wham, Suzanne.

He sat at the kitchen table. Hardly nodded when Irv came in. Tying the knot, tying the noose. His whole body heaved up to the question — "See?"

But what was there to see? Everything appeared in place. Esther managed. The little girl was kept quiet, the apartment was kept clean. Only Babe looked dusty.

"Well, brother. You gonna sleep better with me defending the country?"

Esther came in. Should she be there? Her legs were heavier and her strong arms were meaty. Suzanne was with her. She had started kindergarten that year. Irv had bought her the most elaborate pencil box — it had drawers.

"You see what your niece did in school?" Esther said.

Suzanne came up to him and handed over a finger painting. She had pale skin, hazel eyes, and long red hair. The painting was lime with the slimy white ripples of her fingers running through it. Irv brought her up to his lap. Babe turned away. "Another genius," he said.

"This is very good," Irv pronounced.

She looked at him sideways. She would have liked to believe him, but she had caught her father's tone.

"You can do lots of them at Rose Lake this summer," Irv told her.

Esther looked at him. "You think she should start camp? Isn't she too young?"

"Don't you worry, Esther."

"I don't want to impose on anyone. It's not *my* way."

"What impose?" Irv said. "And I want you to come too. With Babe away, you shouldn't be alone."

"If I had been able to have another one, maybe Babe wouldn't have to go." Esther had enough guilt to go around. Possibly the war was her fault.

Babe said, "Don't blame yourself. I'd rather fight."

She looked at him viciously. "Maybe they can teach you how to do *that*." Then she changed her emphasis. "Irv, tell your brother the army's a job he can't quit."

Irv shrugged. It was unbearable when these two opened up their marriage to him like a spread-eagled whore. He felt like puking. But he controlled himself.

Esther had finished. Suzanne shouldn't see.

Babe sat heavy at the table. He'd grown stout, but not enough to keep him out, just enough to weigh him down. Irv was too big for the Army, but he carried his weight. Suzanne enjoyed sitting on her uncle's lap.

Babe followed Mandy away. Then Irv was completely alone. In the summer his mother and his sister-in-law sat in the enameled metal chairs catching the restrained Pennsylvania sun. Esther knitted. She'd have a concerned, steady look on her face. When she put down her knitting she'd take up her stationery box and write a letter on its top.

His mother sewed. She was the "camp mother" and patched up all sorts of things. When she sat sewing, her legs would spread slightly — up there, somewhere, was her womb.

Suzanne was in a bunk — the Blue Bells, the youngest of the young. All the girls on the girls' side and all the boys on the boys' side called her uncle, "Uncle." She was confused and uprooted. She complained to Irv at first. He explained that at camp time he was uncle to everyone. That was his business. At home, he was uncle only to her. She carried their relationship through the summer like a secret in her heart. She was special to him even at camp, but they must pretend she wasn't. The subtle duplicity thrilled her. Uncle initiated her into the ways of the world.

She was fragile — one of the kids who was forced to drink eggnog every morning — and poetic. No camper. The activity she liked was arts and crafts. The counselor was a painter friend of Mandy's from New York, Snooky Bush. Uncle Snooky. Snooky was tall and thin. He had a pale, unmuscular body that looked silly in shorts and in the sun. His face was long and thin, his eyes seemed drawn and tense. His left eye was glass and unconsciously he was always keeping it in place.

Irv broke the rule of no blood favoritism every Thursday evening at brother-and-sister hour. This was the time, after dinner, that boys and girls could stand on the top of the hill in front of the dining hall and mix. Irv would pick Suzanne out and the two of them would accompany Snooky down the hill, past the girls' side, halfway to the lake, to the arts and crafts shack.

First Snooky would display what Suzanne had done that week. He was teaching her to draw. Then Uncle would ask to see what Snooky had to show for himself:

Rose Lake Lake
Self-Portrait of a Clown
Sabbath Services.

Small canvases, oily brush, bright colors.

Irv stood at the long wooden work table while Snooky held the canvases up.

"Ya see what I'm playing with here, Irv? Watteau's clown. Ya never saw it? Over there." He had it pinned up. Painters pay homage to the past.

Snooky was all over the place explaining. He had a real pedagogical streak. Mandy had hired him impulsively, but he had turned out well.

Snooky talked and talked, like an Indian dancing around a fire. His energy went into words that circled the essential flame.

After their visit, Irv and Suzanne would continue down to the lakefront. They'd sit on the wooden bleachers and watch the oncoming night blemish the water.

"You know what this camp is going to be someday?" he asked her one night.

"What, Uncle?"

"The best."

And after he'd walk her home to the girls' side, he'd go back to the shack for a long talk with Snooky.

He bought his first paintings that summer:

Rose Lake Lake
Carnival
Mess Hall mit Kinder
Boys' Side, Two

for $125.

S. Berman Bush threw in some sketches too.

❧ ❧ ❧

After the war, Mandy stayed in Italy for a while. He wrote Irv the most ecstatic letter. He was *ready!* He had kept notes. "Good," Irv wrote back, "enjoy." He wondered about Mandy's book, for he realized now that Mandy hadn't the extraordinary powers of concentration and self-discipline of, say, Snooky Bush, or — of Irv himself. There was a streak of fluff running right through Mandy; when the winds blew, it ruffled up this way or that.

Irv poured everything back into the camp. He stayed in Pennsylvania half the year and, with the strong country women and a few stray men, he built.

During the war he had set up a small guests' dining room, so that on "parents' weekends" the parents who stayed in neighboring towns could eat at the camp. The food was good and plentiful. Irv had his connections. Right after the war he built a guest house on the grounds and did away with "parents' weekends." Parents were welcome any time. By the season of '46, while Babe was still in Oklahoma, Esther fell into her first job. She was needed in the camp office to keep the parents' bookings and billings straight.

Babe came back the following fall, around his birthday. He was young again, spare and vibrant. Irv rejoiced. The mother gave a birthday dinner: everything he liked to eat topped off by a mocha cake from Batz. Babe patted Suzanne and told her to blow out the candles.

Irv got his brother a job with a kosher wholesaler. For the first month Babe preferred to walk to work. He felt like a high-school kid starting a new term. He could smell the tang of football season in the brisk air.

Irv took him shopping for clothes. Suzanne didn't pester him. She spent her time downstairs keeping busy with grandma, waiting for Uncle. Babe was so relaxed he played newlywed with Esther.

For a while.

One day the following spring, while Irv was supervising the extension of the guest dining room, he saw a man walking across the meadow. He knew the walk of that man like he knew his own brother. Mandy approached him lovingly, as if he had brought the mountains and the blue sky and the spring day with him.

"Irv!" he called and straight from Italy he threw his arms around him and kissed him on each cheek.

"It's good to see you, Mandy," Irv said when they stood once more on equal ground with their own skins between them. "You look fine."

Mandy looked sure of himself, in control. He wore a light gray suit with a wide waistband and a buttoned fly. His white shirt was opened at the neck. His kinky hair fringed around his neck and ears, and his mouth didn't shiver with excitement when he spoke. He had a funny, open-mouthed smile now — very knowing. He looked at Irv with sheer delight. "I missed you a lot, you son of a bitch," he said.

"Come on," Irv said, putting an arm around his shoulder, "let me show you around."

"So this is what you've done by yourself," Mandy repeated as they walked; but it was Irv who was more deeply impressed. Mandy was having his own thoughts. Irv remembered these preoccupations as if they were yesterday.

They had dinner that night in the village near the camp. The Point L House serviced the farmers for miles around, but it was a weekday night and they were alone. The owners made a fuss over Mandy. Mandy was still Mandy. When people smiled at him he caught the smile and whizzed it back. They ordered steak sandwiches, French fries, cole slaw. Mandy drank beer, Irv coffee.

After dinner Mandy read to him.

He read about sailors on a boat and their captain. The men were as real as the two of them sitting there, but their motives were small. Irv was terribly upset during parts of the reading. The captain was a disgrace to America. The sailors on leave in Naples were no better than pigs.

Irv watched with amazement as this horror and destruction was recited softly through Mandy's steady lips. The worse curses, the actions of whores, treason, flowed through these lips that could smile at anyone who would smile back. Irv became enmeshed in the web of Mandy's lies and for minutes at a time he struggled to disentangle himself as the narrative went on.

"Had enough?" Mandy asked finally and paused. He gave Irv that slack open-mouthed smile.

"This is what you've done," Irv said slowly.

"Oh, there's more," said Mandy, mistaking Irv's emphasis.

"Well, let's order some dessert, then read me more."

Warm apple pie, full of cinnamon, vanilla ice cream melting into it. Mandy read again.

It struck Irv, in the middle of a quiet philosophical passage in which the narrator wonders about the fate of men, that he was listening to something incredible. These were the High Holy Days and Mandy had found his name inscribed among the living. He read out loud from the book of life.

It no longer mattered to Irv that he did not like Mandy's book. Strangely enough, he never did. It was only when he saw the movie (the opening — heroic chords and a panorama of the sea, with the big ship and Mandy's name coming into view) that he felt again that swell of emotion he had felt at the Point L House listening to Mandy read.

"That's as far as I've gone," Mandy said. "Of course, I've just given you the highlights."

"You got much more to do?"

He shrugged. "Who knows? With luck, I can finish up soon."

"What's luck?"

"A quiet place to work. I've had it! I need some time alone."

"Why don't you stay here?"

"Listen, Irv, I know I've got a camp to run..."

Irv cut him off. "No. *I* can do that. That's not what I meant. Stay here and write. Write all the way through the camp season for all I care."

Mandy looked at him greedily. "Does that mean you like what I've done?"

"I believe in it, I'll tell you that much."

"So do I, Irving, so do I."

"But one thing — aren't you going to mention the Jews and the concentration camps?"

"Why, in God's name?"

"That's what it was all about."

Mandy hooted. "Jesus Christ! Next you'll tell me they fought the Civil War to free the slaves."

Mandy took room and board at Joan Anna's farmhouse. Joan Anna worked at the camp. She was a strong, handsome country woman. She had the barbed, no-nonsense manner which reminded Mandy of certain Neapolitan women he had known. But the room was clean; gauzy white curtains with polka dot nubs speckled the meadows. A bed, a desk, two chairs, wooden pegs for his clothes, and a wooden floor that looked rough from scrubbing.

"Isn't this great?" Mandy said to Irv. "Here I'm a monk."

"A Jewish monk," Irv reminded him.

"What other kind is there?" Mandy unpacked his typewriter onto the desk and went on retreat.

Mandy, the spirit of Camp Rose Lake. Slack-mouthed, absent, he roamed through that camp season. He visited his business; he worked in Joan Anna's room. On Thursday nights he joined the salon: Snooky Bush, Mandy Mershheimer, Suzanne Bender, Irv Bender, at the arts and crafts shack. He interceded for Suzanne so that she could remain past her hour. He had a special feeling for the girl because of her father's eyes. He knew something would go askew; when it happened he thought "so that's it" and from then on believed he had known it all along.

He promised himself, Irv, and the whole world that the next season he'd work like a bastard. But the next season at Camp Rose Lake never came. He was in New York haggling with his editors, getting things done right. And the following winter *Warship* came out.

Irv opened his presentation copy: To Irv Bender, who brought me luck from the beginning — With the love of the author — MM.

The printed dedication said, simply: *to carlina.*

"Who's Carlina?" Irv asked.

Mandy shrugged. "Someone I knew in Rome," he answered through half-opened lips.

"I thought you were in Naples."

"So I was. But I was in Rome too."

He said no more.

Irv asked no more.

But he heard his mother's voice in his head: In this world, trust blood.

For Mandy, one thing followed another. By spring he was in Hollywood working on the script of someone else's book. Irv quipped, I couldn't ask for a silenter partner.

❧   ❧   ❧

And the camp grew. Eventually even the young lawyers from Greenspan's had bellies and kids to send away. The people in Jersey City who'd never had a dime now had used-car lots and concessions, sporting-goods stores and haberdasheries. People Irv had known all his life decked themselves out, glittered like new pennies.

All except Babe. (Or that's the way it seemed to Babe.) He didn't make a go of anything. He had been sent to college in a good suit and had been able to put his hand in his pocket and feel change. Now all the slobs from those days had bulging back pockets and fat asses. Oh, Babe looked as good as any of them, Irv saw to that. But Babe was getting nowhere.

Irv got him this job and that.

Nothing.

Esther got a job in a lingerie shop on the Square and stuck with it except summers when she worked at the camp.

In the summer, when she and Suzanne went away, Babe stayed home.

But in the fall or winter or spring he'd go up to camp and futz around. He didn't call it work. He put no disguise on the fact that his brother supported him. He didn't give a damn if the whole world saw. "See!" He was out of whack. Wherever he was, he'd look slowly around. Where was he?

Irv thought he looked pathetic in the Pennsylvania hills. He walked down a dirt road as he'd walk through the Port Authority Building, suspicious, vacant, alone.

When the weather was good he'd sit on an enameled chair in the sun.

He painted the laundry with Joan Anna. He began to stay at her place. To certain women, Babe was honey.

The two brothers were at the lake one chilly spring night. The stars gleamed and through the dark they could see the depths of blue encircling them.

"She's a good sport," Babe said.

"What does that mean?" Irv asked.

"I'll tell you, brother. A woman who enjoys it and then lets you forget about it is a good sport."

"Do *you* enjoy it?"

"Do you?"

"Not really. It makes me sick. But then, I've only known whores."

"They're all whores."

"You talk carelessly for a man who has a wife and daughter."

"Carelessly," he mimicked.

Somewhere in the dark night, Irv's eyes rested on the fact that Babe had a mother too. But this was unformulated. It remained the dark outline of the buoyed raft in the distance.

"Jeez, Irv, don't get sore. What the hell do I know?"

"You know you married a woman you respected."

"The worst kind. Put a ring on their finger and they turn into animals."

Irv shivered at the bitterness in his voice. "Esther's a good woman, a strong woman. And she loves you."

"Love! God help us! Never marry a woman who loves you. She'll rub your nose in it!"

"Oh, I'll never marry anyone. I never thought I would and I never have." He said it as if he was aware of how strange it was for a man to stay true to his intentions. "I'm a freak."

"Some freak! You're better than the rest of the world put together. I know."

Irv smiled into the dark. "I'd give a lot for you and Esther to get along — if only for Suzanne and Ma's sake."

"You want me to stop shtupping Joan Anna, do you? Just like that?" He snapped his fingers. "Eventually, brother. All comes to he who waits." He had a flask with him — his father's habit. He took a swig.

❧ ❧ ❧

One day Esther walked from the lingerie shop to the Trust Building on the Square where Irv shared a suite with a lawyer. Esther had "decorated" his corner; she looked at him behind the desk approvingly, as if she had placed him there. Her body had thickened and she had revenged herself with Pan-Cake make-up, heavy blue eye shadow, and light brown, reddish-tinged hair. She poised on the brink of middle age — almost eagerly.

"Can I treat to lunch?" she asked. "I'm a little shook."

Greenspan's had moved to a new corner and had redecorated. After they ordered she sat back and sighed. "Poor Abe Hess, he's got a cancer good."

Irv's nod acknowledged death at a distance. "So what else is new?"

"He wants to put everything in order. Now that he knows there's no chance he walks around the store taking inventory. A real mensh that one. Upmost in his mind is to provide for his wife and children." Her eyes gleamed as she said that, as if Abe Hess's deterioration exemplified reality, which had inexplicably, cruelly, passed her by.

"Looks like I'll be out of a job," she said. "Abe Hess wants to settle his estate."

"He's selling?"

She nodded.

"What's he asking?"

"He's asking for an offer. A place like his is worth something for the name and location. He's a reasonable man. He's just looking out for his family. Not to leave loose ends."

"It would be a good deal for someone," Irv said.

They looked at each other.

"Have you spoken to Babe about this?"

She smiled, more at Irv's use of her husband's name than at the question itself. To hear her husband's name was to remember a big joke — played on her. Of course, the question, too, was funny.

"Speak to Babe? Me?"

"Well," Irv continued, ignoring as usual the ragged edge to her voice, "I'll think this over."

"Fine." But she was so excited by her idea that she could not let it drop. "A little store like that makes money. *That's* what to think about."

⚜   ⚜   ⚜

The mother sat on the sofa with an intensely abstracted look on her face. When Babe's fate was at issue she consulted the gods. Esther sat straight. Her nerves played with her eyes, but she would not budge. Irv was serious, superior. Suzanne sat with them as well. She was not too young for this kind of serious business. Babe looked around him. Here, as ever, was the audience for the drama of his life.

Irv had the papers in front of him. In slow, exact sentences he reviewed the contract. It included a clause that would pay him back. Babe asked him to repeat that section. It intrigued Babe, gave him a glimmer of himself.

When Irv finished, no one spoke. Babe realized they were waiting for him. He felt, within the exactitudes just stated, up to a response. It was a sure thing. You didn't have to be a businessman to see it.

"This time you'll have luck," the mother said with all the conviction of her love. "This time Irv's found you something good."

"Me running a mama and papa store," Babe said. "How does that strike you, *mama?*" he asked Esther.

She ignored his sarcasm and said with great feeling, "You'll never regret it, Babe, I promise."

"I won't? Then it'll be a first."

Esther looked anxiously at Suzanne, as if to alert Babe that she was in the room.

But she didn't have to worry. Babe liked the idea. He had recaptured the old illusion of his respectability.

"You gonna help us in the store, Suzanne?"

"Oh yes!"

"Well, if the kid'll work too, I say, why not? Let's get these papers back to Abe Hess tomorrow. Before he's six feet under."

So Babe went into business. He walked among the bras, the girdles, the Suspants, the hosiery, the slips. There was always one sale table on which stiff-nippled bras, snagged panties, grayish girdles, odd-sized slips were put to be picked over. It was the only heap in the store. He enjoyed watching the women fuss over it.

A man in his business is supposed to be as neutral as a gynecologist. Abe Hess had been a natural. To him his stock was "merchandise," his customers his "livelihood." A new regime with Babe. He joked, he commented, he observed. At first Esther thought she would die. But it worked out. Women liked Babe, who was not antiseptic like poor Abe Hess.

And Babe liked Babe. He walked in his own store among his own things. For the first time in his life he made real money, and he made it the way he had always wanted to, without any effort at all. With his charm and Esther's work, they raked it in. The store did even better than it had under Abe Hess. For a while his old irony failed him; he enjoyed being in ladies' underwear.

But times changed. Gradually the profit began to dwindle. Babe no longer felt as smart as good luck had made him.

Right across from them a huge discount store was being built, and along the highways, in small places you never heard of, people were running like sheep to shop.

Esther said, "We should open in the Acres of Paradise they're building."

"Lay off, will you," he answered.

But she wouldn't quit. "Well, if we stay here, we must change the complexion of the merchandise."

She talked like she knew something.

Who was she, suddenly, to know something?

For the first time shvartzers came into the store. She was changing the complexion, all right.

He knew his luck had run out. One day his eyes ran over the bras, the girdles, the slips, and Suspants on the rummage table and over the new line of cheap housedresses like the ones his mother used to wear and he realized these things were someone else's spoils, they had nothing to do with him.

Behind the counter he saw Esther, her back to the nylon stockings which were shelved as neatly and categorically as ever. He no longer enjoyed watching her open a box of stockings as she did now, dividing the tissue paper and running a careful, capable fist into the gauzy thigh to show the shade to a customer. He was ready to lie down and die, and she stood there determined and accurate, her fist in the nylon stocking.

She would not admit that they were through on Journal Square, two imposters in Abe Hess's store. She made her sale instead, and then, when she saw he was staring, she smiled at him. None of the old expectancy in her smile. They shared, suddenly, the ultimate intimacy and for the only time in his life he really wanted her. The moment passed as a chill of fear came over him. As far as she was concerned, he could drop dead. Her legs, now hidden by the counter, thick, slightly varicosed, sensibly shod, would walk over his grave and go on.

A few weeks later he was standing in the store like a business-man, his right hand stroking his left elbow, when he felt a lump. Cancer. Abe Hess had infected him.

He left the store. Hung around the Y again. Ran for the bookie. Took baths. A lump appeared at the side of his neck. It became difficult to talk. He nodded, he grunted, he stayed longer and longer in the steam.

The lump in his neck flattened, but one appeared in his knee. Sometimes just walking along the streets of Jersey City, tears would roll down his cheeks.

Esther had her last act of martyrdom. She moved into Suzanne's room and left him the bigger bedroom for himself. Was it martyrdom? Her eyes shone with pleasure when she told him.

Having the room to himself was a blessing. He stayed in it. He drank. It was like being in the steam.

Irv came in one day. Opened both windows, sat at the foot of the bed.

"Let's talk, Babe."

Babe looked at him.

"Tell me what's wrong. Aren't you feeling well?"

Babe shook his head.

"Well then, what hurts?"

Babe pointed to his knee, to his elbow. Irv reached over and felt the lumps with his big hand, tenderly.

"You seem to have bumps."

"Cancer."

"When's the last time you've been to a doctor?"

Babe shrugged.

"You stop worrying about nonsense," he commanded in his imperial business manner. "We'll see a specialist and get to the bottom of this. I'm relieved. You've been brooding about nothing. You'll see."

Sure he saw. The doctors reassured him. Just the beginnings of arthritis, not cancer at all. Arthritis at his age? For a while he believed them. He wanted to. Irv spent a lot of time with him, driving him around. Babe began to talk again.

"You'll be back to work in no time," Irv said.

"No," Babe answered. "There are spooks there. I won't go back."

"What about Esther?"

"She's the chief spook."

"You know, Esther thinks the two of you could do business in a shopping mall. Look how well the Acres of Paradise has been doing in a short time. You could lease a store. Something exclusive. Not the discount trade at all. What do you think?"

"I don't give a shit where she goes or what she does."

"Babe, it's your business. I bought it for you."

"I'll be like Mandy then, a silent partner."

"You've got a family to support."

"*You* do, brother. I'm going to die."

Irv changed the subject. Babe often said he was going to die. Irv often changed the subject.

Esther wouldn't give Babe a cent, and he didn't want to take from Irv. The few years of success had ruined him. He kept up his errands for the bookie.

Irv wanted him to spend the summer at camp. To recuperate.

Babe stayed in Jersey. It was a steaming summer, so the tears rolled down his cheeks like sweat. The lumps reappeared in his neck. Along the front of his legs he could feel the bumps spaced like vertebrae. He lived downstairs while Irv and his mother were away. At night he could hear Esther's legs above him.

He ran into trouble with the law. Somebody's wife who didn't like the numbers put the finger on him. He was brought to the station and questioned like a thug. Then they let him go. Was that the end of it?

Maybe they let him go because when they questioned him he broke down. Maybe they didn't like to see a white man cry. They were all on the take anyway. The questioning had to have been a formality. Was it?

He was such a little fish. If they needed an arrest, they could well afford to make an example of him. Or if they didn't need a patsy, maybe they'd try to put the screws into his rich brother.

Every time he saw Esther her eyes said, "Criminal." Now she left him money. He was in disgrace.

When Irv returned from camp he couldn't believe his eyes. Babe had become thin and shaky, sweaty and abstract. He tried to talk but he mumbled and made little sense.

Esther let him come back upstairs for Suzanne's sake. But Suzanne merely stared at him in fear. The only words he had ever had for her were insults and commands. Now she couldn't make them out at all.

Irv made the round of specialists with him again. He'd open the door for his sick brother and usher him in to magical places. In Irv's Caddy, in the specialists' waiting rooms, even in the art galleries Irv stopped at, the smells of leather or rubbing alcohol or paints were alluring. Irv drove, specialists examined, dealers sold with such confidence in their ability, such certainty of their place. This was the world Babe had been expected to experience. This neatness was all.

Nostalgia gnawed at Babe's heart, tears welled in his eyes. Here was the dream worth dreaming. Why hadn't he had the ability to reach out and hold on to a steering wheel or a stainless steel table? Why hadn't he insisted on walking on a thick soundproof rug? Weren't these things more substantial than the mist in his heart and the bitterness in his soul?

Esther! he realized, was what he had reached for when he was young. She was the machinery he had tried to grasp. Fool! Fool! He had been stupider than the others. That's why he had failed. Yet looking back to Greenspan's years ago, to Irv and Mandy Mershheimer and the Danish on their plates, to those two — his now-rich brother and the now-famous writer whose name he sometimes used — still, their motives seemed unreal to him, shadowy, unsubstantial. He did not know, did not understand, how they kept on planning while a St. Vitus's dance was coursing through Benjamin Bender's soul, while he was being claimed by the blind mother, life.

The specialists disagreed.

Arthritis?

Lymph node inflammations?

One guy said there were no lumps.

Babe suddenly had an eerie surge of power. They were mad, he realized, despite their lavish boxes, their shining instruments. They knew nothing. He knew everything. He was the expert. He was going to die.

Then he felt very, very sad. All these professionals would go on with their magnificent lucrative madness, knowing nothing, while he who knew everything was going to die a hideous death. Lumps would crawl over him like spiders. His own flesh would be devoured. His bones were already coming closer and closer to the surface. He felt them ready to crack and burst through.

Irv was concerned about the weight loss. Back into the big car, back to New York.

Babe mumbled to one doctor that he tried not to touch his own skin at all. This was a weight man, not a skin man, so he took no account of Babe's words.

One Monday the following April, in midafternoon, Irv was packing to go to camp. He had just gotten up; his waking life stretched farther and farther into night. His mother was out. Dead quiet. He didn't hear Suzanne come in from school, only became aware of her when he heard his own front door slam open.

By the time he got to the living room, she was slanted backwards against the door jamb, her legs quivering, her pale skin deathly, sweat tearing at it. Wet strands of her disheveled red hair stuck to her face. She saw him. She tried to move. She couldn't. She could only point her head upward. Her mouth opened. She meant to scream. But she belched. A dull raspy rattle came from her throat. Her head jerked downward and she began to vomit.

He ran past her and up the stairs. The front door was open and so was the bedroom door. A hunk hung from the ceiling in there. Irv walked to the doorway, tripping over books on the way. It was a dangling corpse with some obscene thing jammed in the middle of its face. He stared at the thing, his own small eyes wide open to the burst white sockets he saw. He stared at the thing until he understood it was his brother's tongue.

❧ ❧ ❧

Mandy arrived too late for the funeral. He got there during the week the family sat. Esther and Suzanne were sleeping downstairs, so late that night he and Irv went upstairs to talk.

Irv sat in the living room of the haunted place. Mandy set down the half a platter of 3-D sandwiches from Greenspan's which Esther had sent up with him. "Get him to eat," she had whispered hoarsely. Irv had not slept and he had lost weight with the first shock, so his face was haggard and his eyes were wider than before. Both he and Mandy stared for a moment at the gay red cellophane tips of the toothpicks that speared the bulky, soggy rye bread wedges. Mandy picked up a sandwich. "Like old times," he said and bit in. His tone was fraught with secret meaning.

Irv looked up at him. Mandy had a wise, knowing look in his puffy eyes. He had shorter hair; it wasn't as kinky. He wore a white silk shirt, monogrammed, but his sleeves were rolled up carelessly. He had put on a few pounds (who hadn't?) under his alligator belt. He was more bulky, more world-weary, more knowing. What did he know? Could he show Irv something more than the squalid, hideous death?

"My front door had been opened," Irv began. "He must have unlocked it, come in while I was still asleep. I slept while he stood over me. I could have stopped him."

"Same Irv," Mandy said. "Still your brother's keeper."

"I have no brother to keep."

"You'll find another."

"My brother's dead."

"He left you a child. You're a father now."

"Suzanne — I'm her uncle. That's enough. Leave me in peace."

"She found him?"

"You should have seen him, dangling, an animal's tongue sticking out of his face. It wasn't Babe."

"Who was it?"

"Some thing. Not a man. It was not Babe."

"Yes it was," Mandy said softly. "Babe's dead."

"Tell me, Mandy, what does it all mean?"

Mandy didn't answer.

Irv said, "How could Babe have done it?"

"Were there any hints? Did he say anything?"

"No. He was afraid he had cancer. He was *afraid* of death. Who would think he'd do this?"

Mandy's look became too knowing. Irv didn't like it.

After a while Mandy asked, "I heard downstairs there was a little trouble with the law?"

"He was afraid of that too."

"Unjustifiably?"

"It was nothing. He dwelled on things," Irv said slowly.

"He was playing with rough boys."

"I thought of that. But it's impossible. They wouldn't have touched him. He was too small a fish, insignificant. He took his key and opened my door and watched me sleep before he did it. If he had only woken me up! No, he did it himself."

"I always remember him at Greenspan's that night, before he married Esther. Remember, Irv? Someday I'll write it down. Those eyes of his, those big blue eyes. And his crazy desperation. He died in front of us that night, I think. We watched it together years ago."

"Nonsense!" Irv cried out. "Crap! Don't make one of your stories out of my brother's death."

"What else is there to do with it?"

"Make sense."

Mandy looked at Irv. Had he made this effort, traveled these miles to stare into blind eyes?

"Is that what you asked Babe to do too, Irv? Make sense? There is no sense, Irv. Babe made no sense. He made no sense for many years. Years ago I knew he made no sense. You still don't know. All these years and you still don't — oh, forget it!" Mandy stopped himself.

"What do you mean?" Irv asked. "What don't I know?"

"You don't know that Babe made no sense. That he couldn't make any sense. Babe was out of his skull."

"No!" Irv cried. The word came so quickly, so loudly, that he himself realized that that "No!" had been within him all these years. Now it was too late to hold it in. He didn't have his brother to protect. He let the word go and tears came after it. He surrendered to love and to pity. He cried over the wretched corpse of his eternally vulnerable brother. And he cried over the enormous failure of his own love.

Mandy had shown him more.

❦ ❦ ❦

Two years later, in the late spring, Mandy came back to Jersey City on business.

Irv had moved to the Boulevard; he had a penthouse that overlooked Lincoln Park. The mother let Mandy in. She was shrunken and her eyes were watery and she treated Mandy like she saw him every day.

"Irv's waiting in the park for you. You didn't see him?" Mandy had come the other way.

"Come, look out." They went to the window. He could see the graceful bronze statue of Lincoln, the tender grass, Irv with his back to the building, waiting on a bench. This was the only splendid place in Jersey and Irv had come to it, at last. Mandy moved from the window and stood in the room with the mother.

Her words for once echoed the look she gave the world. "See how much we have now, Mandy? We have nothing."

The living room was eerie and exquisite. Its style was eastern. There was a rich, large Oriental rug in shades of blue on the floor and round it many exotic plants that made green predominate. The walls were artfully crowded with paintings; the furniture was plush, leathery. The mother in her robe did not belong. In the old days she had wanted riches. Now she spit them out in her surviving son's eye. What did she know from decor? What did she care?

She wanted to go back to her own room, back to the TV. "Go, Irv's waiting," she said and turned her back and left.

He found Irv on the bench. The two of them sat facing the Madeline School for Girls. Suzanne went there now. Irv had immediately transferred her from the public school.

A group of little girls in blue gymsuits and white knee-socks were in rows, exercising under the direction of two formidable teachers, in the section of the green park reserved for them, the elite.

"Suzanne will be glad to see you," Irv said. "You've been very kind to her. She saves your letters."

"Does she really?"

"Why not? They're worth money."

"I'm worth so much that I need more."

"Never do business when you're hungry."

Mandy laughed. Things couldn't be better. He was starting all over again. His wife had agreed to a lump settlement. Then he would remarry. Wash the slate clean. Start all over again.

Irv said he might be better off paying alimony. After all, a big house and a big lump all at once might not be good business. But what was business to Mandy? What Mandy needed was right in front of his nose. He saved his overviews for his novels. All that mattered was the money from the camp, half of it under the table, tax-free, and the load off his mind. *Warship* was being made into a movie. He had no worries for the future.

The spring day blended with his expectations and his nostalgia. "All I want is that bit of cash and I'm out. I leave the rest up to you. But one thing I'd like to feel — if things change for us in some strange way, if I'm ever aching — that I can have back in."

Irv looked at him through half-closed eyes. "That won't be in the contract."

"When did we ever need contracts? As long as it's in our hearts."

"What heart?" Irv asked. But he couldn't fake it. He knew Mandy too well. Irv was getting off cheap and Mandy was going to make him pay.

So he nodded. A very half-hearted nod, before the school let out.

"Here they come now!" Mandy said, satisfied and excited. He saw Suzanne, tall, fair, virginal in her alien uniform of blue. Picked her right out. "She must be a great consolation to you," Mandy whispered. "The daughter we never had. I bet you feel like a father now."

Irv looked beyond the children and answered slowly. "To the extent that I wish she had been a son."

PART TWO

"One-Nine-Five-Nine at Camp Rose Lake. No other year the saaaayyyme." He stood at his living room window listening to the song the campers sang as they rushed from the mess hall. He watched the girls ready to start down the hill, many of them linking up, clasping each other behind the back, arm around arm. The wider the chain the better; then they studied synchronization of steps. The boys seemed older, wiser, meandering back to their bunks on the west side of the hill. Both boys and girls wore green shorts and green polo shirts with the circled gold monogram CRL on the front. The steady color added perspective to the view of scattered children. "No other year the saaaayyyme."

His broad face was immobile, except for his eyebrows which were raised slightly, answering some intelligence. He was forty-eight years old, another birthday. He tried to remember his boyhood birthdays. But he only remembered Babe blowing out the candles. The memory filled him with pride. There were rich brothers who sent their kids to this camp who didn't talk to each other because of a small in equity in a father's will. But what was a birthday cake between him and his brother? Irv only wished Babe two birthdays a year.

Irv thought he understood now how monks end up in cells, artists in garrets, great thinkers in greater isolation. In no less a way had he and his mother become wed to her sublime limitation. But he couldn't keep up with her. Her private maid, her separate quarters, her Florida winters, her older son's constant attention to her comforts in no way mitigated her endless stare into the damp dug grave of the son of her womb.

38

Whereas with Irv, the concentrated devotion only lasted as long as he could look in Babe's eyes.

He looked down at Babe's oversized star sapphire on his pinky. He remembered buying it for him years ago. Something of Babe still winked back at him from the gaudy blue.

He planted trees in Israel. He founded a scholarship. The Benjamin Bender Award. In print it didn't look like Babe at all.

He could not believe at first that she would be right, that gradually he would no longer remember. And finally he forgot.

She knew it would happen. It was her pleasure.

The beautiful face, the tinted high-school graduation picture that his mother perpetuated became the powdered head of a corpse. But no doubt when she spent hours staring at it, she saw Babe.

He pretended as long as she lived — as long as the sorrow, the moaning, the oy vaying, the indiscreet parting of the withered legs, the unclean old-lady smell permeated his life. Then she died quietly in her sleep. Such an unexpected and unworthy end to her long agony of grief. Irv felt she had spited him, had taken her last opportunity to cheat him.

Her companion found her. "Your mother's gone to rest, Mr. Bender," she told him softly.

"See?" he heard, a whisper from the bedroom. "A lot you know."

Then she took Babe with her and left him alone.

That spring, when he looked down from his window onto the gleaming statue of Lincoln and the green grass and the Madeline girls' ordered play, he took in a deep breath and expelled the past. What had been, disappeared. So quickly, so easily that he soon felt a quiet more overwhelming than any he had known. For he could not deny the reflection of his inconstancy in his mother's eyes.

He tried to save himself from life. He tried to die. Or, as the comedians of the day had it, get married. A marriage of convenience. For companionship. He believed he saw such relationships all around him. That's what he thought of human nature. He believed the women who ran after him were only after his money. That's what he thought of himself.

"Gold digger" his mother had called Tootsie Sachs, a widow in the building who had paid him a lot of attention. She had asked what she could do for him after his mother died.

Platinum hair, platinum jewelry, long, white, mother-of-pearl nails. Vivacious, vacuous, good-natured. Tanned all winter long.

He invited her to go out to dinner, but got a headache instead. She'd come over and cook for him. After all, he'd already sent his own girl home. He was too sick to argue, took aspirin and went to bed.

When he woke up, she was sitting there beside him, concern plastered on her face.

"Better?"

He was.

"You know what you need, Irving Bender?"

"No, what?" He *had* asked, fully aware that there were few needs she could fill and that she was advertising for herself.

He was still slightly cottony from the aspirin. Maybe she'd answer: A wife; a companion. Maybe he'd say: Why not? They'd go eat.

But she said, "Even more than a home-cooked meal, you need a woman."

Her face took on an expression of fearful seriousness. She brought her long, tanned hand to her ruffled chiffon blouse and began to unbutton the satin buttons.

"Please, don't. You don't have to!" he said.

She ignored him. Took off her blouse, took off her skirt. Then the bra. Finally the panties. Like a strip show.

Thin as she was, her skin sagged over her muscles. Her black bush hit him in the eye. She was oblivious to her absurd appearance, in a delirium. She knew just what to do. He had a rare glimpse into the mysteries of womanhood that had always mocked him from behind his mother's eyes.

He was passive and would not move, had never moved, and she knew all about him. She opened his robe, opened his shorts, and that greasy mouth worked on his penis. He couldn't treat her like a whore. He could have shot right into her mouth, but he controlled himself.

She stopped, swung her skinny leg around him. She was excited. She was actually enjoying herself. She stood up and straddled the mound of his stomach. She took her hands to her vagina and spread it, bent her legs a bit so that he saw her vulva sticking out at him. Then she sat on him, closed her eyes, and began to rock rhythmically, slowly, slowly, as if she had a child in her arms and then faster, faster forgetting her arms, the child, the way her small shapeless breasts flapped. He was so transfixed watching her that he gave her quite a ride. He finally recalled what was expected of him, closed his eyes, and came.

She screamed as if it had been she who had come, then slowed down, stopped, and tried to come into his arms.

"Won't you hold me?" she whispered, cajoling as she dismounted.

"Get out of here," he heard himself answer slowly, then he rolled over and went back to sleep.

When he awoke he thought with relief it had been a wet dream — until he smelled her.

In the kitchen he found a pathetic note on the top of the foil that covered the food gone cold. "I want only what is best for you my love, Tootsie."

He took another look at the couples he saw around him. And he knew what he did not want.

He drove up to camp along country roads, through quiet towns. Strangers seemed to line the streets for him. His heart joined the spring day. His eyes filled with tears. The back of his throat itched to agony. He felt blessed relief.

He picked the site for his summer house that day. At the flat top of the hill, plenty of land around it, but in view of his office and the dining hall. Where he stood now, under the log rafters he had pitched so high that he fit in place.

He fit in place at Rose Lake, certainly — in the locale the stragglers from the mess hall now lauded in song: "The Pocono mountains, where the punch runs out of fountains, that's Roohose Layache."

But where in One-Nine-Five-Nine was the wine of life?

He heard the static clicks of the microphone and Larry's husky voice. "Good afternoon, parents. Luncheon is now being served in the guests' dining room."

Irv glanced at his watch. Larry was early with the announcement. He was going to drive to the airport to pick up the famous Mandel Merschheimer. Irv didn't go on such errands anymore.

"Mr. Declaration of Independence" his sister-in-law called him. Her birthday card had arrived a day early. It had a teen-age girl on the front with a heart-shaped body and eyes as big as her breasts. Inside it wished him everything nice and many, many more — *underlined.*

He saw Larry walking briskly toward the house from the office. He wouldn't have loitered even if it had been any other day. Just a little too much sun and his skin freckled and peeled. Irv himself had rubbed Noxema onto those arms and legs — gently. He knew how to handle things of value, especially when they came to him bruised.

He walked out of the house to greet him. "Here're the keys to the Caddy."

Larry looked up and smiled.

They had fought last night. Irv wanted him to go to the airport in the camp station wagon. It was better on these roads. Why the hell did he need the Caddy? Now he put his arm on Larry's shoulder and whispered, "Get some gas and take your time. Mandy'll wait."

Larry smiled happily, knowingly, raised a finger to his forehead in a mock salute and was off.

"Drive carefully!"

The car's horn turned Irv to the road once more.

"Happy Birthday!" Larry called after him as Irv shooed him away.

❧ ❧ ❧

Larry had walked into Irv's small office at Journal Square two years ago.

Lean. Like a lot of GI's were the first months after they got out. Their sparse physiques made them look alien in the land of plenty.

Tense. Picture the everyday world as a continuous escalator — moving stairs, up, down, up. And you have to jump on and believe in what you don't see — an exit sign marking your floor.

Polite. You've got to make the right impression. Why is it that so many people who don't know the first thing about themselves are convinced they know what others expect from them?

"Sit down," Irv had said. "What's your name again?"

"Lawrence Driscoll, Mr. Bender."

"Tell me something about yourself."

"Well, I spent four years in the marines as an enlisted man. I traveled widely in the East. Now I've returned to civilian life and have enrolled at St. Peter's College in a commercial course. I have my GI bill, but I thought I would qualify for a part-time job such as you described."

"You have a family to support?"

"Sir?"

"Are you married?"

"No, sir."

"Engaged?"

"No, sir. I'm not emotionally involved at the moment."

Irv smiled. After the incident with Tootsie, he had learned to accept his cruelty.

"Well, Lawrence — is that what you're called, 'Lawrence'?"

"My friends call me Larry, sir."

"Well, Lawrence, what are your qualifications?"

He blushed. He had very pale, very white skin. As he rolled off his memorized skills, Irv looked into his vacant face. Irish. Dark hair. Light blue eyes. Large mouth kept tight. A small nose, once busted. Cleft chin.

He wore an inexpensive but new charcoal-gray suit. The collar of his white shirt was irritating his Adam's apple. This was the only flaw in the anonymity suggested by his dress, his carefully controlled face, and his crew cut.

Irv glanced at his watch.

"Am I keeping you, sir?"

"No, I've got all day."

He asked a few more questions. Heard out the innocuous answers.

Cat: Question.

Mouse: Answer.

Until the cat struck.

"What high school did you go to?"

"Lincoln."

"How come you avoided mentioning it?"

"I completed my studies in the service. I entered college on the basis of the high-school equivalency test."

"Why did you leave high school, Lawrence?"

Larry leaned his head back and sighed. Irv saw his Adam's apple rubbed raw. When he looked at Irv again his whole body had relaxed — slackened, out of spite. He smiled at Irv, loosely, carelessly. It was all over.

"I was put in reform school, for fighting with a teacher. He tried to make a fool out of me *too*. I knocked *him* out."

"You think I'm trying to make a fool out of you?"

Larry stood up. "I know it."

"You leaving? Don't you want a job?"

"Are you going to hire me?"

"Sure."

Irv had surprised himself surprising Larry.

The few friendships Irv had had in his life had begun magically:

Mandy

Snooky

A painter named Shapiro.

These men didn't sit down alone. They brought with them infinite possibilities, clues to the riddle, more.

Larry Driscoll sat down a stranger and he brought nothing Irv could value.

A mess.

A waste.

A college course that could only get him a job.

An Irishman, ready to slug it out in a world of Jersey City Irishmen.

That night Irv had a vivid dream. Larry Driscoll's extraordinary cream-white skin which chafed so easily took on personality, became the whole chameleon, did its own dance, *was* Larry Driscoll. Who needed him?

Irv.

It was the way the boy could concentrate on what was in front of him, a row of figures, a counter of shirts. He would look up from a menu. Slowly his eyes would focus on Irv's. "More? What are you talking about? They've got everything here."

Irv brought him home. He had a place to bring him to now. Home.

Larry talked about his early life in the same self-obsessed, factual way. Irv began to wonder if you needed a mother who really loved you in order to learn how to feel really deprived. Larry's mother hated his jovial, irresponsible father. She loved her son Larry in a way he translated into a terrible burden. Everything she needed she threw on him and he had thrown it right back in her face. He threw away a lot that was good in him, that could never be reclaimed. Ironically, that part must have been airy, for his burden grew heavier and heavier.

Now he hardly ever saw her. It would shock Esther (indeed it shocked Irv) that he never even sent a card. "Why should I?" he'd ask. "Did she ever show up on a visiting day?" Case closed.

In the same bitter matter-of-fact way, he'd pick out a closet queen for Irv, or an adulterer, or someone on the make. You see? You see? There you have it right in front of your eyes. The nature of things. Something slithering, snakelike, secret.

Life was a secret society of the initiated. Sex was the initiation. As in any fraternity.

A lifetime of whore mouths and wet dreams. Larry couldn't understand how Irv had lived all those years without realizing he was gay.

There was a malicious streak in the way Larry brought him out. You see what you are? I saw it all the while. I walked into your office and I knew it by the time I sat down. You were trying to make me. Then you tried to make me go away. But you couldn't, could you? And we'd still be sitting in your living room wondering if the moon were blue cheese if it weren't for me.

Irv was the man who tried to make a fool of him, who could still throw him out any day. But it went on. Larry could say any thing, act any way. Irv was there.

"Where have you been?"

"None of your business."

One night Larry came to Irv's very drunk and answered his question. Irv slapped him red across the face. But he didn't throw him out.

It was a very rich life after that, basketball games, business, dealers, Florida over the holidays, camp on the spur of the moment and in the summertime.

As Irv thought about the last two years, his eyes fell on a small Shapiro. It recalled the volatile artist and many conversations through the night. The heart of Irv's collection had been an accumulation of all the afternoons he had had with time on his hands and all the nights he had listened to young men plan, philosophize, joke. Those times were fewer now. Larry didn't like the evenings with the younger artists, the heart of Irv's collection. He preferred meeting the Big Names.

These were the guys who lived well and needed money. Irv, waiting for Mandy, realized he didn't know a big-name painter who was as bad a businessman as his old friend. They had had to deal with too many dealers and collectors right off, they had been screwed too often when they were young. The abstract intensity of their youth had gradually fastened on the thing they made. Its worth in dollars was alchemy enough for them. This magic substituted for the old dance around the fire of the soul.

They cost and Irv paid. But never top dollar.

And Irv could see Larry loving every minute of his calculated and ironic negotiations with the Big Names. In Weston, Connecticut,

Larry experienced the magical enjoyment Irv had felt years ago, sitting at Greenspan's, talking with Mandel Mershheimer.

The long ride to the country. Dinner with outspoken people, a visit to a splendid studio on the grounds, then brandy — cognac, armagnac — by the fire.

The first time Larry had become self-conscious, formal, devious.

On the long drive home Irv spelled it out. If you don't know something, ask. Being stupid is pretending you know what you don't know. Being smart is only having to ask once.

Larry asked once. He discovered people were happy to answer, to tell him, gratuitously, that they had just found out the day before yesterday about a wine, an omelette, a place.

Irv would look at him across the table. See? That's how easy it is. All it takes is one slight scratch below the surface.

On the way home, Larry would often cut deeper. He maintained his special talent for seeing sex silently transpire.

⚜   ⚜   ⚜

"Uncle?" Irv heard at the door.

"It's open."

Suzanne came in.

She was tall and her torso was broad like Esther's but her hips were not large and her legs were slim. Standing there in her green shorts and shirt she gave the impression of being a big flower on a long fine stalk. A dahlia, perhaps, with her reddish hair streaming about her face and shoulders, and her speckled eyes big as Babe's. Yes, a dahlia because it is so startling and varied, and because it shared with her skin the potential to flame or to pale. Yet a dahlia, unlike a redhead, is never homely, so Suzanne had the larger range.

"Is Larry with you?"

"No."

"He's not in the office either. He must have left already. I wanted to go to the airport too."

To meet Mandy? To be with Larry? Irv wasn't sure.

"It's not your day off."

"I could have gotten away."

She could have. She wasn't a counselor in any strict sense. She taught arts and crafts and bunked in Snooky's old shack.

The rules were relaxed. Why shouldn't she be special? Irv could afford her.

"Did you eat lunch with the camp?"

"Yes."

"Well, come keep me company anyway."

"Sure."

They walked out into a beautiful day, the sun and clouds high, a breeze blowing. It was very quiet. Rest hour for the campers. Hushed, tinkling lunch for the guests. Murmur of flies: *hizzzzzzzzzzzzzzzzzzzzzzzzzz.*

They passed right by the Oak Room, the guests' section of the dining room, to the back of the building and mounted the stairs to the kitchen.

"Look who's here!" said Joan Anna who was sitting by herself at the long table by the door, drinking coffee and reading a movie magazine.

She was wearing jeans and a white polo shirt through which you could see the outline of her bra. Her bleached blond hair was in pigtails. The style clashed with her tough, angular, sunburned face.

Country woman and cynic, she was head of the camp laundry now.

Orson, the chef, was busy with the guests' lunch; one of the boys set up for them.

"I hear Mandy's comin'."

"That's right," Irv said. "He wanted to stay at your place."

Joan Anna smiled. "Like old times."

"I told him you were a bride again. Still on your honeymoon."

She laughed.

He looked at her with an affection based on the passing of time. She had slept with Babe and when the morning came, got out of bed and went on about the day. She could say to Suzanne, "Oh yeah,

I knew your father pretty well," and she could be around Esther without blinking an eye. When her second husband died, she found another. She went on. Like the waters.

"When Mandy gets here," she said, closing her magazine, "he can tell me all about the stars."

"Why do you waste your time reading that junk?" Irv asked.

"I'm a student of human nature," she said, stretching, and then straddling the bench, ready to stand. "Did you find Larry last night, Suzanne?"

(She was looking?)

"No," Suzanne answered awkwardly. "And I missed going with him today."

"You shouldn't keep that boy out so late," Joan Anna said to Irv as she rose. "He has to get up in the morning to earn his living."

"I need you for advice?" Irv called after her.

To Suzanne he said, "I don't want you hanging around Larry."

"Just because he isn't Jewish?"

"That's for starters. I've got a business to run here and I don't want you turning the heads of the help."

"Larry's head's not turning. He has a one-track mind."

"I'm glad to hear it. I don't need your crushes."

He sounded like her mother. "What do you know from love?" Esther would ask if she hinted at any feeling. Esther had played for keeps. A widow for years, she watched her daughter zealously, waiting for Suzanne to knock her flat.

"You want to look at real love? Then look at all your uncle's done for you!"

"Oh, Uncle. You treat me like a baby."

He look surprised. He always gave her enough to do whatever she wanted.

❧ ❧ ❧

Mandy walked out of Irv's car, to his front door, into his arms. Smiling. Oblivious. "I'm back!"

He brought some of L.A. with him. His hair had been straightened and was browner than before. His body was tough. Health clubs were coming in. Bicycles that went nowhere, walks one didn't take, Olympic pools that paced you line by line, Swedish saunas stark and proud that replaced the old immigrant, the shvitz. Under Mandy's Italian silks, Irv felt muscle.

His face had aged. But a good tan covered the beginnings of ruin — a romantic ruin, full of nuance and shadowing.

"Where'd you find that kid?" he asked, pointing at Larry by the car. "He drives like a bat out of hell. You teach him?"

"He learned that himself."

"What are *you* teaching him?"

"The business."

"So that's the Larry Driscoll everybody's writing to me about."

Irv raised an eyebrow. Like much of Mandy's hyperbole, this reference could be reduced to one source — in this case, Suzanne, who carried on the old correspondence.

"I hear —". Mandy was distracted. He saw a woman waving, running, her hair wild in the breeze she stirred. He left Irv, ran to meet her. They were in each other's arms.

Then Irv knew Mandy was in trouble. His eyes were red when he came back with her.

"*This* is who I came to see!" he said, holding on. "This is *our* life, hah, Irv? *Our* past all grown up and ready."

"Ready for what?" Irv asked.

"Larry," Suzanne called. "Can I see you for a moment?" She left them and walked toward the car.

Irv's reaction was cut off by Mandy. "Leave the kids alone. They got something brewing."

Irv looked at him. The same Mandy, always ready with more.

But it turned out to be a false alarm. Suzanne returned with a package. "Happy Birthday, Uncle."

Irv opened it up. It was one of her small water colors, newly framed. Larry had picked it up in Scranton.

Irv nodded noncommittally.

The work reminded Mandy of Suzanne. Texture, pale washes, surprising violet and fuchsia surges against sea-colors of calm.

"Hey, that's great," said Mandy.

"Why so surprised?" asked Irv.

❧ ❧ ❧

By the next morning Irv had the eerie feeling Mandy had never been away. He found him at the outdoor Sabbath service. It was a beautiful day; the golfers putted in the meadow; the children sang. From a distance their young voices called, "Come O Sabbath Day and bring / Peace and Healing on thy wing..." Irv walked over. The rabbi stood behind a draped podium leading the song. His wife played the piano. Two old-timers faking in the new world. She had one eye that rolled as she banged out the melody in spastic imitation of the real thing. The rabbi made grandiose movements with his mouth. You could hear his Yiddish accent and children giggling under the song.

There was Mandy in the last row on the girls' side at some solemn rite of his own imagining, singing, "And for every troubled breast / Grant Thou the Divine behest / Thou shalt rest / Thou shalt rest." He even wore white.

When he saw Irv he got up and joined him.

"You sleep well?" Irv asked.

"Did I ever! But what the hell are *you* doing up in the morning?"

"Weekends." Irv moved his head in the direction of the golfers. Everywhere you looked there were parents. Twenty-five dollars per person per night and try to get a room on a weekend.

Sixteen bunkhouses on the girls' side.

Fourteen on the boys'.

Average ten a bunkhouse at $650 each.

Ten guest houses.

How many rooms each?

Figure. Everyone figured. At times the whispers rustled through the air.

"What a business!" Mandy exclaimed.

"I can't complain. But what's with you? You suddenly getting religion?"

"It can't hurt. Anyway, I thought I'd see Suzanne."

"Well, she's right —" Irv looked around. "Funny, I thought she was here. Well, come on. The mountain will go to Miss Mohammed."

Mandy turned once more to the fields and the putters. He said, "I remember Babe stumbling along where they're playing golf now. Looking like he was offended by the country air. I guess it must have been fall or early winter. Nothing was green."

"You remember?"

"Like yesterday."

"You really do, don't you? What was he to you? But you painted your own fancy picture and you still see it."

"What do you see?"

"Sam Levitt and Gus Traubitz in Bermuda shorts. Nothing. I can't even remember what Babe looked like. Or Mama. They're like this." He crushed the grass into the dirt.

The piano and the Sabbath song rose louder.

"We're all like that," he continued.

"Like dirt under your shoe?"

"What else? We don't care. We don't remember. Only ourselves. We do all right for ourselves in the long run."

"I'll tell you something, Irv. You've done all right."

"Have I? I have my compensations."

"Such as?"

"Come, let's walk." As they walked down the road Mandy seemed intent on walking back into the past. What was so good about it, Irv wondered? What did his old friend find there?"

"Jeez. The whole damn girls' side is new," Mandy said when they came to it.

"Why not?"

"Have you noticed there's nothing left in this whole friggin country? Either its brand new or some ruin waiting to be demolished."

"The arts and crafts shack's the same."

"How come you haven't built a new one?"

"Suzanne won't let me."

"A girl after my own heart."

"The shack and the girls' recreation hall across the way. When I do one, I'll do the other. I'll do them right someday."

Irv never did. One-Nine-Five-Nine was the year the camp was at its peak. Which meant everyone thought it would get better and better. Though Irv maintained things through the sixties, the shack fell into ruin before he died.

They climbed the stairs to the elevated wooden porch that encircled the shack and Mandy looked up into the encroaching woods that shadowed them as if he were gazing into eternity. Irv was irritated by his old friend's red-rimmed and tearful eyes. And the voice which quavered when he said, "My God, it's good to be back."

Back? Once he couldn't wait to leave.

"You, me, Snooky, Suzanne. Don't you remember?"

"S. Berman Bush. What this place really needs is a marble plaque. You know what he's selling for today?"

"I know *you* have plenty of his stuff."

"Had. Some I've traded off."

"You still see him?"

"Occasionally. Suzanne keeps up her lessons — every Friday at the Art Students' League."

"He was a great guy."

"He never shuts up."

"He never did."

"Now all he talks about is himself."

"Suzanne!" Mandy called. "Hey, I don't think she's here either."

"So we'll wait," said Irv, opening the door.

Mandy sat down on Suzanne's bed and began to leaf through a group of water colors next to it on a trunk. There was no comfortable place for Irv to sit, though he finally conceded to the workbench, with his back to the long table, facing Mandy. "You practicing to be an angel in all that white?"

"Some angel. I'm in trouble, Irv."

Irv took a good long look at him. "Why else would you be here," he declaimed slowly.

"Laura has left me."

Another one gone? This was the guy who was going to marry a good typist. Irv looked at him. The hard build, the rugged face, the eyes that were crying out, the slightly slack chin. "What happened?" he asked. What he meant was, how has this happened to you?

"What happened?" Mandy moaned. "What always happens. Everything turns to shit. That's what happened. You're lucky you never got involved."

"I'm involved."

But Mandy didn't listen. "I'm going to get stuck for alimony again. Irv, my salary's attached. I got a third book started. I can't get another advance on it. I've had it started for four years. *Roman Lives* made zilch. Every cent left from *Warship* is in a house I've had to walk out of."

"Had to? I thought you said she left you?"

"True. I didn't want this."

"Then why did you walk out?"

"What could I do?"

"You could have stayed."

"Nah, she was through with me."

"Well then, you could have stayed and told *her* to leave."

Mandy looked at him. He knew Irv was making sense. And you had to respect sense, acknowledge it, even when there was nothing in it for you. So he gave Irv a sheepish smile, raised his eyebrows, shrugged his shoulders, kept still. Waited for sense to pass like a hero on parade.

"Mandy, don't you ever learn?"

"Learn? You wanta learn, you go to school."

"You *went* to school. You should have taken a business course like Larry. Three wives and you still walk out of your own home?"

"House," corrected Mandy Mershheimer, master of the stunning differentiation.

"So where are you now?"

"Here."

Irv turned his head.

Mandy was silent. Not because the years had yet taught him when to shut up, but because he was frightened. He had always had his big destiny to work out. Looking back he realized he had been lucky. Success came when he was ready for it, and he had accepted it casually as a reward due. But now when he needed it, it receded. And his mistakes were becoming as indelible as his wrinkles. Every day when he looked at his face in the mirror, he realized that tomorrow would come and his face would be a little worse off for it. The scarcely perceptible but progressive drying up of his skin taught him to feel everything he had been blind to in Greek tragedy, in World War II, and in his marriages. Standing at a mirror, before he shaved, he realized his mistakes would no longer dissolve. And he felt terror — well — anxiety.

"And you, Irving? For you things are going better? It must have been an adjustment for you ... being alone."

Irv looked at him once more. "All my life I thought I was alone, but I wasn't. When I was, I was prepared for it. The silence. Better than talk. I took to it."

"It agrees with you."

"Well, it didn't last long."

"How do you mean?"

"Larry."

"I hear he spends a lot of time with you in the city."

"He's agreed to move in permanently. This fall, I'm doing over mama's rooms."

"He's going to move in?" Mandy repeated in astonishment.

Irv didn't answer.

"You know, Irv," Mandy said finally, "an older man, a younger man." He showed a palm of his hand for each. "People have dirty minds. They think things. You should be aware."

"People? Let them think what they want."

"*Is* there more to think?"

"There's more. There's everything."

The fear was on Mandy's face. He had come all the way from L.A. Irv was supposed to be his rock. "You've changed."

"I don't think I've changed. We are what we are."

"Then all those years...I never was quite sure."

Irv smiled. "One thing for sure, Mandy. *You* never change."

They heard the footsteps outside.

Suzanne walked in, with Larry behind her.

"What the hell have you two been doing?" Irv blurted in surprise and anger.

"Swimming," answered Suzanne, just as agitated.

Their suits were dry.

Mandy was embarrassed. This was no place for him.

"Pardon us for not knocking," Larry said. "Well, guess I should get going. Anyone else coming up the hill?" Irv followed him out without a word. Suzanne and Mandy looked at each other for sympathy.

"That's a pretty dry suit," Mandy said finally, "for someone who has just been in the water."

"Hot water," Suzanne answered. She went to her dresser and took out an old shirt — a dress white, it could have been her father's — and put it on over the one-piece black bathing suit.

She sat down at her uncle's place and stretched her legs out to the trunk top. Mandy could see the sparse reddish hairs on her thighs. And then the gold sparkle of an ankle bracelet. He touched that leg. "You shave them, hah?"

"I'm nineteen."

"It's hard to believe."

"Only because I'm treated like an infant."

Mandy didn't know what to say. When she had written to him about Larry, Mandy had answered in a letter full of nostalgia for his own youth, telling her to "experience" in a tone that her grandmother used to use when, her eyes staring beyond the little girl and the food, she chanted, "Eat! Eat!" Well, Mandy wrote to Mandy. To Suzanne in the flesh he said, "Be careful."

"Careful?" she repeated jokingly. "The whole world's careful for me."

"You complaining?"

She withdrew into the world of her most habitual speculation. "I'm complaining that we're a family of celibates."

"Your father did all right."

"I'm sure," she answered, surprisingly close to Esther's tone.

"And your mother had your father."

"And my uncle?"

"Well, your uncle's not completely alone."

"I know, I know. He has me."

Mandy blushed. "Yeah, I guess in a way you have been the center of his universe. You're Babe come up from the ground smelling sweet."

"I'm nothing like my father," she said bitingly.

"Aren't you? *He* had a tongue too. And too much self-pity."

It was her turn to blush.

"I think you've gotten a little spoiled," he said. He understood why. They had made a wordless pact, Irv and Esther, that Suzanne would never again see her father with his tongue stuck out and shit sliding down his pants. Esther's love was the daily reminder of the oath. Irv's clear reign of reason was its substantiation. Babe's suicide had been a tragic aberration in the measured flow of time.

She believed them. But not for their — or Mandy's — reasons. What she had stumbled on that day had been terrible, but not disproportionate. It was something her father would do.

Esther and Irv, reassuring her, reassured themselves; and reared a stranger.

She sat quietly, insulted by Mandy's criticism.

"Hey, Suzanne," he said. "We're friends. I said what I said because I see something very clearly."

"What?"

"That your uncle really doesn't want you to get involved with this fellow. My God, where does a Larry Driscoll come up to you? And —" he raised a hand to keep her quiet, "your uncle's not just thinking of you. He's thinking of himself. He likes that boy. He needs his company. Your uncle's a lonely man. Would you deny him one small selfishness — one small pleasure."

She smiled at him. "Of course not, Mandy." Mandy was frightened once more. For the condescending smile on Suzanne's face was Suzanne's youth running away from him, escaping, leaving him in the stump forest of an old man's convictions. She was as graceful as a fleeting deer and he stumbled frantically through the undergrowth after her.

"Come on, don't clam up on me, Suzanne. It's me, Mandy. Say whatever you want."

"Can I *really* talk to you?" she asked hesitantly.

"My God, yes! You can tell me anything and everything," he exclaimed expansively.

She took him at his word. That's how young she still was. He meant his words. That's how little he had learned.

Now what was there to talk about? It's easier to go through three wives if you insist on talking. Tell me what you *really* think. Tell me how you *really* feel. Mandy had to know. But the fruit of knowledge was not the freedom promised on the incised stone facades of the public schools of Jersey City. The Greek philosophers evidently hadn't known their wives. Nor, would it appear, had they had Mandy's insatiable curiosity.

He was surprised by the freedom with which Suzanne began to talk. But she was talking about first love and first traceable desire and had no idea of the later variations on the themes. Passion was something she felt, something she wanted to express, something she believed would be satisfied by one person at one place at one time — forever.

She moved her legs from the trunk, curled them under her and talked. Larry was different than the Jewish boys and she liked that. He was "mature," he was controlled, he was handsome. He was hard to get.

All of this Mandy found rather easy to take. The banality of virginity did not excite him — as each of the wives he chose amply testified. And he knew himself at least well enough to know what not to ask. So he asked anyway. "Where were you two this morning?"

"Swimming."

"Your goddamn bathing suits were dry!"

"I took mine off," she said, "and swam nude. Larry, not to be outdone, took his off too."

"And what happened?"

"Nothing. Absolutely nothing. We swam."

"The queer," Mandy whispered.

"It's not his fault. He has had lots of experience. He's told me. It's me. I come from a family of celibates."

"Yeah? You pick the wrong man and with a little bit more push, you may end up like the Virgin Mary."

"Don't worry, I'm careful."

"You are?"

"I'm okay this time of month. It's right before my period."

He looked at her and tried to hide his amazement, to stay on her side. But in a way he couldn't keep up. There she sat, as young and clear, as beautiful and blooming as the day, planning what amounted, in Mandy's terminology, to her own seduction.

⚜   ⚜   ⚜

"You'd better get your niece off me," Larry said when Irv had followed him into his small room in one of the guest lodges. He had his back to Irv. "I can't even swim in peace. She knows my every move." He slammed a drawer.

On his free mornings he would go to the shaded cove at a distance from the camp waterfront and swim before the sun got too hot. Then he would sit and relax. The sky was the sky. The lake was the lake. The rowboat passing was specifically manned. He would nap against a tree.

He didn't like intrusions. But what happened happened. He wasn't asking for it.

He turned to Irv. "She's asking for trouble. And if she doesn't watch out, she'll get it! Jesus, she has a lot to learn!"

"Just don't you teach her."

"Then get her off me! I'm no knight in shining armor. You raised a princess, you take care of her!"

"She's not behaving like a princess, throwing herself at you."

"Isn't she?" he asked and paused. He raised his arms as he took off his rumpled jersey. Irv loved him.

Larry went barechested to the mirror on his dresser and picked up his brush. "Sure she's behaving like a princess. She thinks she's doing me a big favor."

"That doesn't sound like Suzanne."

"Doesn't it? Well, she's not going to make a fool of me."

"It's not her fault she has a crush on you."

"That's right, now make excuses for her. But I'm not you. I'm not going to dress her up, give her a fancy name, and then make sure she's nice and protected and that the world stays away. She's your niece, not mine. So you watch out for her. Women. They'll drive me crazy in the long run. You watch out for her!"

"*You* take care of this," Irv answered.

Larry smiled at him through the mirror. "Just like that? And what am I going to tell the princess tonight?"

"Tonight?"

"That's right. She has something *important* to tell me. I'm to see her tonight."

"Don't go."

"I said I would."

"There's no reason to go."

"I told her I'd be there. I'll be there. And I'll tell her to lay off." He turned to Irv. "Or would you like me to be more gentle? Make it easier for her? Or would you like me to screw her? What do you order for the princess?"

Irv didn't say a word.

"This isn't my fault!" Larry cried out in one of his sudden rages. "And when it's over, don't blame me!"

❧ ❧ ❧

That night Irv and Mandy went to the basketball game on the boys' side and then, after taps, joined the parents in the Oak Room. As the song had it, "The new Oak Room / It's not a real oak room / It isn't oak / NO! / It's knotty pine." The blond walls were covered with canvases. Irv had noticed that a lot of painters' wives painted and found out that he could buy Mrs. Big Name for next to nothing. So he did. In 1959, *Parades*, a fabulous suite of huge canvases no one took seriously, hung in the Oak Room. The experts poo-pooed them; they were outside the Benjamin Bender trust. Still, they were colorful and they covered the walls. In the long run they found their market. No one ever went broke seeing what was right in front of his nose.

The parents bunched in, protected from the chill of the night by their warm, expensive sports clothes and each other. They went right for the buffet table set up with coffee and tea and an over-abundance of pastry. Then they sat at the tables, some playing cards, some talking, some of the meticulous long-nailed women knitting, some of the men smoking, staring. The room was noisy, and the nasal north Jersey, New York accents and the short store of Jewish expressions were a comfortable bond of kinship between these people who all had about the same idea of what was gorgeous and what was dreck.

They came up to Irv; they came up to Mandy; they joked, they kibitzed. People were impressed talking to Mandy Mershheimer, of course. He was part of the legend. But Irv was the spirit of that time and place. When he responded to one of them, shrugged his shoulders, gave a look, came out with an enigmatic "nu?" the person was flattered. When he had a few words with a group, the group was thrilled.

Why?

Who knows.

Was it the man himself? His money? His distance? His strangely structured life?

Now that the camp had become so elegant and faultlessly maintained one could say it was the place itself. But Mandy had seen the magic work long before. Mandy wondered if these now-rich people from his old city, who had made such a fanatic and frantic conversion to the surface of things, were impressed by something more than the upkeep. Every other camp was a business. You put something in and you take something out. Camp Rose Lake was a man's life. Irv's spirit touched it, from his own house at the top of the hill to the paintings in the dining halls, to the campers' "sides" and the waterfront. When you walked on Irv's green grass you were in touch with an individual destiny. When you ate the good food, it was as if Irv were waiting with more.

Irv could see the flushes of nostalgia on Mandy's face. And he knew why his old friend was here. But this was no businessman in front of him, this was a dreamer. Mandy turned toward the door each time it opened. And Irv could see by watching him that Larry and Suzanne had not arrived. He touched Mandy's arm when they were alone for a moment. "I'm going home. Want to come?" He led Mandy through the double doors that led to the kitchen, his own way out. In the kitchen, he picked out an assortment of cakes to bring home and covered them with cellophane.

"Remember Greenspan's?" Mandy asked.

"What's to remember? I eat there every week."

⚜ ⚜ ⚜

Mandy knelt by Irv's fireplace and started a fire with too much paper. The flames lept high, then sank. "Turn the heat up," Irv said. Mandy went to the switch and did. Then he stopped to look at a picture — a reclining Venus with waves of paint for flesh. Irv called out the Big Name to Mandy.

Mandy whistled. "Must be an early work, a student piece, before he hit his subject." The name was that of the greatest social satirist of the 30s.

"It's brand-new."

So was the malicious smile on the Titian-like face.

"What did you buy this for?"

"A song," answered Irv, misunderstanding Mandy's question. "He has a new wife. A young one. I bought three of her drawings. He was so grateful he almost gave this away."

Mandy went to his chair and sat down. "Frankly, Irv, I got more on my mind than pictures."

"So what should the pictures do? Fade from the wall?"

Mandy's face was red from the firelight. The constant saunas made it easy for him to sweat. His eyes were almost yellow from the heat of it all. If you saw this man on a subway, on a freeway, at a bar late at night, you'd know he was in trouble. "Irv, I can't go back to California."

"Can't?"

"If I go back I go to jail. I haven't got one penny." Mandy leaned back with a sigh. "I got my manuscripts, some good cuff links, some rotten stocks. I'm in trouble, Irv. Help me. I want back into the camp."

Irv looked at his former partner. He saw the skeleton-dance in his eyes. He longed to be in bed with Larry. With Larry he was alive. With Mandy he was in a past that had grown smoky, suffocating. He was back to a time he no longer remembered, feeling things he no longer felt, involved with values he had relinquished.

His mother once more sat at the table and separated money into piles. Her dry fingers were blunt and wrinkled and oiled in the crevices with the lotion she used. She did not speak, but her lips moved and he heard a buzz between her nose and mouth. Babe slammed in. Irv slipped the kid a bill, his hand on his brother's. The mother looked up, saw, chose not to, returned to her chore. Irv looked around. The kitchen needed a paint job. He'd get that done too. His mother awkwardly and carefully tied the money he allotted her into a wrinkled handkerchief left over from Sol.

"You went off to the war without telling me. You wanted your own way in the world. You'd let all three of your wives make mincemeat of my property without blinking an eye."

"Why are you bringing up the past? What's finished is finished. I gotta begin again."

"Begin again? All you need is to put on your sailor suit to be everything you were and everything you'll ever be."

"What the hell are you talking about?"

"The past. Not *your* past, my past. The way it really was. You'd be better off going away and writing another *Warship*, talking about the war again, forgetting the Jews. Why not? You've forgotten you're a Jew."

To be called no Jew by a Jew who was no better a Jew?

What did Irv mean? What's a Gentile? What's a Jew? What's a Swede, an Armenian, a Greek? In America it's that little bit salvaged that sets you apart. That makes you one with a few.

Irv's words meant more than he could ever say. They meant that Mandy had walked off the porch and forgotten him.

The look on Mandy's face: innocence, amazement, hurt. What Have I Done To Deserve This? "Irv, I beg you, come out in the open. Tell me what's bothering you!"

"You are, Mandy, you are. If you are a writer, why not go away from all of us and write? You've done it before."

"I told you, I don't have a cent! How far can I get on cuff links?"

"We'll see about that," Irv said, slowly, deliberately, in control once more.

Something awful appeared on Mandy's face. Irv had seen the look before. Desperate hope that Irv meant more. Fear to press him further. Mandy rubbed his eyes. "I need to think."

"Take your time. Have a vacation. You're my guest."

Mandy had come to find Suzanne's uncle, Babe's brother, his old friend, Yetta Bender's son. He had written books about how everything ripples by, but he had made a deviation for that rock, Irv Bender. And like all sentimentalists, his syrupy oversight had a little something in it for himself.

They heard a car drive up. "That's Larry," Irv said. "Right on time."

"On time?"

"I told him to be back before midnight."

Larry came in, his hair still wet from a combing, his face whitening in patches from pale rose.

"Did you have a good time?" Mandy asked.

"Good enough. Excuse me, will you? I'll just leave the keys and go, Irv."

"No, stay! Mandy's getting ready to leave."

Larry shrugged his shoulders and walked into the kitchen to get himself a drink.

Mandy said petulantly, as he got up to go, "I'm surprised you haven't moved him in here."

Irv walked him to the door before he answered. "Here I run a business."

❦ ❦ ❦

Mandy had planned to go right back to his room, but he found himself walking down the hill instead. The night was cold and he walked fast. And he didn't keep a thought in his head, which was a blessed relief.

He meant to knock softly on Suzanne's door to test if she were awake, but he saw the flickering candlelight and yelled, "I'm freezing out here. Are you decent, Suzanne?"

"Come on in."

"Hey, you'll freeze," he said.

She was lying over the covers in a long pink nightgown. He threw her her less glamorous wool robe. The candlelight came from a cluster of the campers' newly made candle holders in the middle of the work table.

"Did I wake you?"

"No, I was just thinking," she said, sitting up in bed. He could see her breast fill up under the soft material. She stood on bare feet as she wrapped the Scotch plaid robe around her.

"How did it go with Larry?"

"Crummy." She sat on the bed and Mandy sat next to her.

"You've been crying?"

"No, no. Swimming ruins my eyes. Gets them all bloodshot."

"If that bastard's hurt you, I'll —"

"No, Mandy. It's not his fault. He's been in trouble before when it hasn't been his fault. I don't want to cause him any trouble."

"What kind of trouble did he get into?"

She paused. "I can tell you can't I? But don't even let Uncle know you know."

"That goes without saying."

"When he was in high school he had an awful experience. His homeroom teacher was a pervert and Larry didn't realize it. The man kept inviting him over and helping him with his homework — all sorts of things. Then he tried to do something perverted with Larry and Larry fought him. And he ended up in reform school, although nothing was his fault at all. That's why Larry's always suspicious. He refuses to trust anyone at all."

"And you believe every word of that?"

"Mandy! What are you saying? Larry confided in me. He didn't have to! It scarred his life. He told me that sometimes, as good as Uncle has been to him, he wonders what Uncle wants in return. He can't trust anyone."

Mandy got up. Walked to the table. Watched the candles glow.

"I wish I could make it up to him," she whispered.

"Better you take his example and not trust anyone." He wanted to tell her the truth. But he couldn't take the responsibility for it.

"You mean he's a liar?"

"Things aren't so black and white in this world, Suzanne."

"You don't like Larry, do you?"

He shrugged and moved back to the bed. "I don't like him upsetting you." He sat down. "What happened tonight?"

"Nothing."

"Well that's something."

"Is it? Maybe it just means that there's something terribly wrong with me. I'm a freak, aren't I, Mandy? My mother asks why I don't become a real counselor. Go live in a bunk. Make friends. But I don't have much to say to any of them."

"These people," Mandy said offhand. "This place. Sheep in a sheep's pen. All they care about are the outsides of things. They do what they see being done. The New Jerusalem. Irv knows what they want. He's turned this place into a show place. Everything so clean it squeaks. And nothing going on. No horseback riding anymore. No archery. I counted only four canoes. It's not a camp anymore, it's a container. You're in the only real place left. Don't doubt yourself. Doubt everyone else."

She smiled. No one else talked to her like that. They told her she should change.

Mandy said, "It must be better at school." She had just finished her first year at Barnard.

"Well, when you live home, you don't get to join many things. For me it's rather like a glorified high school."

"Didn't I advise you to accept Mount Holyoke? I knew it. Why the hell didn't you go away to school? You were going to."

She shrugged, looked guilty.

"Jesus Christ!" Mandy moaned. "You stayed to moon around that shmuck! Chrissakes, sweetheart, there's a whole world full of men more interesting, with more to offer than Larry."

"Like you, Mandy?" She meant it.

"Better, much, much better than me."

"I don't believe that," she said softly. She shook her head suddenly. "You know, maybe I really am insane. I'm crazy. You should know what goes on in my head."

He put his arm around her, stroked her hair. "Just relax, baby. Stop thinking for a while. Tell me about tonight."

She rested against him, stared past him at the flickering candles.

All afternoon she had helped the young campers with their ashtrays and candle holders, and at general swim she had stood duty on the dock. But all the time she hadn't been there. No, she hadn't been there at all.

"Right after taps I did something spooky," she told Mandy. "I took a shower. Not in the senior bunk. I walked across the road to the old shower house under the recreation hall."

When she had been a camper, everyone had used it. The whole bunk would enter that dusky place which was lit through small oblong windows that touched the ceiling. As she washed, she thought of her old counselors disrobing with the girls. She remembered Cheryl Stober's wide circular breasts that didn't stick out at all, that clung to her chest like suction cups, tits dead center. She remembered Honey Perloff, the most beautiful counselor she had ever had, with the face of a pallid angel. In the shower she was as hairy as a satyr. As Suzanne rubbed her soapy hands over her body, under her arms, in between her legs, rinsing and washing again, warding off any possibility of stench, of offense, she recalled the secrets of others. The shower house had been the house of mysteries when she was young.

"What's so spooky about taking a bath?" Mandy asked into the silence.

"Oh, it was eerie all right," she answered finally. "Washing alone, at night, in that huge place. I thought, if Larry found me here, he'd be scared to death."

"That's for sure," Mandy said derogatorily.

"Larry's right," Suzanne said. "He says you don't like him and he's right."

"When did he say that?"

She had walked naked across the road, back to the shack. She had combed her hair and lit the candles. And then, obeying her intuition of Larry's sensibilities, had put on a nightgown.

"Tonight. When he got here he wanted to know why I had asked him to come."

"That seems pretty obvious to me."

"I told him I wanted to give you and Uncle a chance to talk together. I asked him if we couldn't do the same. I asked him to sit where you're sitting now.

"He came over and sat down and asked why he should help you out. He said you can't stand his guts.

"I told him to bring his complaints to you, not me, that you were a pushover for the truth. He put his arm around my shoulder, sort of patted me, and told me how smart I was."

She was quiet then. After a while Mandy broke into her reverie once more. "I'm to believe that you spent the night discussing me?"

"Oh, Mandy, it's too embarrassing to talk about! Nothing happened, that's all."

"You never have to be embarrassed talking to me."

She looked into his eyes. "Well, I kissed him. Then I did something else and he pulled away and asked me if I wanted to get into trouble. I told him it was impossible for me to get into trouble tonight. He told me I didn't know what I was talking about. We ended up discussing the matter at length."

"And then?" Mandy asked cautiously.

What was there to tell? She had stretched out on the bed finally, said she was tired, and asked him to kiss her goodnight. He had lain down beside her and put his lips on hers. He didn't move, just lay there for a long, long time. "Oh my God," he said suddenly, looking at his watch. Her uncle had bought him one of those damn things that glow in the dark. "It's almost twelve." She asked if he were afraid of turning into a pumpkin, but he didn't think that was funny. He had to bring back the car. "Don't worry," she told him. "I'll take the blame if you're late." But he got up, went to the bathroom to wash, and then rushed out.

What could she tell Mandy? She put her hands out in front of him. They held nothing at all. "He didn't want me."

"He's crazy, not you," Mandy whispered.

"He didn't want me."

Mandy was silent for a minute. Then he asked, "What did you do that he said would get you in trouble?"

She was quiet for a moment and when her voice came it was husky. "I put his hand here," she touched her breast, "and — I put my tongue in his mouth."

"Suzanne." She looked up. Without warning, like a slap across the face, Mandy kissed her hard on the lips.

He held on to her. "Why are you freezing up, Suzanne? Do you only want what you can't have? I want you. I need you more than life. Let me have you!"

"Mandy!"

"Don't be scared."

"Let me go!"

"Sure," he said. She sat straight up. "I didn't mean to scare you," he whispered hoarsely.

"You…you, surprised me, that's all."

He took her hands. "Look at me," he said. Then he let go of her hands. He untied her robe slowly, gently. "I want you, Suzanne." He put his hands on her barely covered breasts. "I'm mad about you."

"Are you just saying that to make me feel good?"

"You *are* crazy," he whispered. "Kiss me," he said. "Do what you did to Larry."

"Mandy —"

"Go ahead, sweetheart. Do what you did to Larry." His lips parted. She moved closer. And then without any awkwardness at all, met his lips and found his tongue.

It was happening finally. He pulled her nightgown up over her head and then brought her down on the bed. He sucked her nipples and stroked her. She fondled his hair as he made love to her breasts. Then he kissed her stomach and raising himself, kneeled between her legs and undid his fly and pulled down his pants. He lay on her again. She felt his tongue circling her nipple, his fingers rubbing her, till one went into her vagina and moved. "Relax," he whispered and she did and then two fingers went in and she began to become excited. "Touch me," he begged, directing her hand. She stayed above his underpants for a long while, and then, by herself, reached for his penis. "Just hold it, don't move," he said and pushed his fingers further up her, moving her more and more. "We're gonna make it the first time." He got up and quickly took off his pants. Kneeling once more, he opened her legs and placed them around him. He put his hand on his penis and directed it in. It burned. He stayed there, then went further and he burned her again. He got it all the way in and moved slowly. She was terribly uncomfortable, as if she had just contracted a fever. He came. She felt better. He stayed in her a while, resting, and then withdrew and used his hand on her, the way she did it herself, until she came.

He raised the hand for her to see. There was blood on it. For a second, until she realized, she thought it was her period.

"Don't worry, sweetheart," he said when he woke up and saw her watching him. "It gets better. The first time is never too good, and believe me, believe me, it could have been much worse."

He went into her again and moved back and forth, gently, slowly. It was not as uncomfortable, though neither came.

Then they propped themselves up and looked at each other's naked bodies through the soft glow of the candles. "How long have you wanted me?" she asked.

"Since you walked out of the Madeline School in your blue uniform."

"That's awful!"

"Don't I know it."

"Why did you take me today?"

He couldn't help smiling. "You want a reason? So Larry Driscoll wouldn't get you first. You'll never stain his nuptial sheets."

She giggled despite herself and put her head back, resting it against the rough wooden wall.

"Do you want to marry me?"

"Never," Mandy said with sudden seriousness. "Never."

"Even if I fall madly in love with you?" She realized what that meant after she said it.

"No danger of that," Mandy answered drily.

She took hold of his penis. "Are you sure?"

"Don't be coy. It's me, Mandy."

"We're such good friends," she said from her heart.

"Yeah. You might not need enemies."

❧   ❧   ❧

Esther Bender usually came to the camp every Sunday, after the weekend crowd thinned out, and stayed until Monday night. She had missed last Sunday, figuring Irv and Mandy would want to get reacquainted. She wasn't one to butt in. Anyway, too much vacation and she'd go crazy.

Lord and Taylor's kept her sane. She had worked in Better Dresses since she'd sold the shop after Babe died. What does a woman alone need with headaches?

She needed to keep busy. To improve her mind. Although, had she had a different daughter, one who confided, she'd have taken off more time.

As it was, she lived with her newspapers, her radio commentators, and her 9:30–2:45 job. She knew where they began and she knew where they ended, and she spent every bit of energy that she did not lavish on Suzanne informing herself, peeling off the meat, right down to the bone.

She broadened the basis of her set opinions. Politically, she squared with Max Lerner of the *Post*, and on all the issues of the day she was with the radio commentator Barry Gray — the last voice she heard late at night before the bits and pieces of her life unglued and she drift ed into the horrors of her first sleep. At Lord and Taylor's she smiled at everyone, but she sided with the position of management. The help didn't know from aggravation.

She believed in her set of values and her own common sense. And her brother-in-law, Irving Bender.

She'd go crazy sitting in Jersey City playing Mah-Jongg all day long or being pampered at the posh beauty parlors by Mr. Joseph or Eduardo, or any of those fairies who played like women were poodles. Let Irv do for Suzanne, that was his pleasure.

Esther did for herself.

She had few friends and no enemies (Yes, sure, she always said, and went her own way).

She only prayed for the essentials.

Her daughter should grow up and marry a man with a set of values. The grandchildren should be healthy. Esther should live to see them grow up.

What else was there?

Who else was she, but Milton and Sarah Schwartz's daughter.

A rich man's sister-in-law.

Suzanne Bender's mother.

Grandmother of a generation yet unborn.

She had somehow worked herself into harmony with vital statistics. If her views were not exactly biblical, it was because the Bible mixed nonsense with sense. She didn't need a glass of wine to swallow a bitter pill.

She sat in her brother-in-law's office now, waiting for him to speak. When the two of them were silent together she thought they shared the past.

Something was up, Esther divined.

What, she couldn't say for sure.

But whatever, she understood.

Here was a man. More than a man. A personage.

Here was the living proof against all the impulses of youth.

Years ago, would she have given this brother a second look? Never! Her head was stuffed with nonsense. What did she know from a mensh?

Suzanne shouldn't have to learn the hard way.

"And Suzanne? Is she still mooning over Larry?"

Irv shrugged. "Mandy's keeping her busy this week."

"I feel reassured." She put her hand against her heart as if she knew something. "She respects him."

"He doesn't have a cent," Irv pronounced slowly from behind his desk.

A tremor of nervousness passed over her face. All Esther ever wished for was low tide, for she stood on damp sand, facing the ocean. After her hysterectomy she had sprouted a deep voice and a noticeable moustache, both of which she had trouble keeping under control. Her voice was often a harsh, confidential whisper. And, in her solitude, she often grabbed her hand mirror and plucked out a hair. Her face was pale and she wore only enough make-up to look neat. Her short teased and lacquered hair was a shade too red, but the color kept her clean of gray. A good dark green sports outfit from her own department stiffly contained her spread, no-nonsense body.

Mandy broke? So that explained his visit. She remembered the promise between the old friends. It was a story by now, a part of the Camp Rose Lake waterfront and the good food and Irv's money. Her brother-in-law and the famous author had parted like blood. Mandy gave the camp to Irv by letter and Irv had told him he could always come home. She clipped those words from one of Mandy's interviews after *Warship* won the Academy Award. Even Irv smiled as he read, although he had never breathed a word. "It's incredible," Esther said. "Not a cent? He had everything. How could it slip through his fingers? This you don't need."

She herself believed in the legend. "Listen," she said, "don't worry about us. We got plenty. We don't need all we have. Do what you think is right. Just consider yourself."

"That's exactly what I'm doing."

Her smile said sure, sure, sure. Then she looked at him more closely. "Has he asked to come back here?"

He put a finger to his lips. "What Mandy asks for and what Mandy gets are two different things."

She felt strangely dissatisfied, ineffably let down.

Larry's voice came to them as a whisper through the door and megaphoned through the window: "Good afternoon, parents, luncheon is now being served in the guests' dining room."

"That's us," Esther said and started to stand, but then, slowed, as if she had momentarily forgotten her body and then felt its tug and had to make allowances for it. The look on her face was slightly disgruntled. She walked a few steps before she fully straightened up.

She and Irv left the office and walked slowly toward the Oak Room. Larry rushed ahead, clipboard in hand. Irv watched him disappear. He felt annoyed at his sister-in-law, as if it were she who was holding him up.

But of course they'd both have to wait for Suzanne anyway. They saw her walking up the hill with a man. She was in white shorts and wore the counselor's weekend V-necked black vest over her long-sleeved white blouse. She was barelegged down to her Capezios. Her hair was pulled off her face, but hung loose.

The man wore tan shorts in the full Italian cut and a green Italian knit jersey tucked in. He was also barelegged and he wore what men did not wear at Camp Rose Lake, leather sandals.

"My God!" said Esther. "My eyes are playing tricks. That's Mandy?"

Who was he kidding, she thought. Would muscles make him younger? He was older than she.

"My God, Mandy. You've grown into a young man," she said in greeting. She would never have been derisive to the Mandy that should have been. And she had no idea she was being derisive now. They embraced and she saw his lined face and bit her tongue not to ask who his hairdresser was. Who was he trying to kid? He had become part of the cheapened world.

Thank God for Irving Bender.

"Bubeleh," she said to Suzanne and kissed her. "How do you like my little girl?" she called to Mandy, just to find something to say. Suzanne thought she'd die in her mother's arms.

"I like her fine," said Mandy steadily. "But she's no longer a little girl."

Suzanne smiled appreciatively and escaped her mother.

And she gave Esther a look. She threw her sex right in her mother's face.

Esther's eyes lit up. She moved, stalked them.

She knew.

And she knew what she knew.

Thank God it only lasted a few steps. Then she pushed it out of her mind. Completely.

"Did you read about the little tramp from Short Hills?" she asked them. "Just disappeared. Drove her parents *crazy*. Then they found her in Chicago. Amnesia, they all claimed. Well, I thought different. Sure enough. Turns out she just wasn't in the *mood* to get married. A nice big debutante wedding and all those nice gifts were too much for her *nerves*. She wasn't in the mood to grow up. Better to make a fool of that swell young doctor and kill her parents."

"I see," said Suzanne, "she owed it to her parents to get married."

"Wait, you wait," Esther turned her out-of-control voice on her daughter. "Wait till you have a daughter of your own before you get so high and mighty!"

"It'll be a long wait," Mandy said.

Suzanne giggled.

"Let's hope so!" Esther hissed at him and then turned to Irv.

"But you are all out of the world up here. No reception. You know me, I never turn on a TV. But I sat glued, glued. Khrushchev and Nixon fighting like women in the kitchen. The Kitchen Conference they're calling it. Bickering. Statesmen they're called. Yelling at each other in front of the whole world. Did you see the Macy's ad? They showed the American kitchen that all the Russians are crowding to see in their park over there. Underneath the picture the ad says, 'This could be your kitchen.' In fact, yours is even better, Irv. And in Russia they're all scrambling to see it, and Khrushchev is jealous and yelling at Nixon in front of it. What we Americans take for granted! We're spoiled. We are all spoiled."

"Politics," Irv said. "Eisenhower has just sent Nixon to Russia to set him up to run for president."

"That's exactly what Senator Humphrey said," extolled Esther. "But do you know, as much as I hate that bum Nixon, I swear Khrushchev was really jealous. *Jealous.* Why our workers live like kings in comparison. Khrushchev couldn't *believe* the houses we have for them here."

"He should see them lined up, row after row after row. Right, Irv?" Mandy asked his old friend.

Irv felt a splash of embarrassment. "Have you been following the papers?" he asked Mandy.

"Nyet, as the Siberian kid said when Pat Nixon offered him chewing gum. That's the only part that interested me. Esther, was it on TV?" He did a mincing imitation of Nixon's wife: "I just don't understand. Julie and Tricia chew all the time."

"Come on now," said Esther, laughingly, all smoothed over. "Don't tell me Mandy Mershheimer doesn't follow the news?"

"Why should I? I used to write it."

"Same old Mandy," said Esther, not quite believing her words.

When they entered the Oak Room, every eye turned. Suzanne bustled past Larry as he tried to seat them. Then Irv held him back, to go over details.

Mandy, Esther, Suzanne, smiled this way and that. Irv didn't. He was the omniscient overseer. The guests were gratified just having him in the room. The Boss. When people called him Uncle, that's what they meant. And some of the parents called him Uncle because they didn't feel comfortable saying Irv. As he stood now, face to face with Larry, everyone in the room believed something important was being imparted, something that meant money.

Perhaps it did. Passion itself was suddenly subordinated to the expert management of the room. Larry demanded the most extreme professionalism from Irv.

What Larry loved, passionately loved about the man, was his huge success. It was bigger than life — or else, Irv carried it off that way. A star. Larry's desire was to hitch on to it. Irv's success mystified him, made him grasp, stirred him to reach farther than he had tried before.

When the big man humped over him, entered into him, Larry came in ecstasy. He was beyond everyone. When he awoke, he was the same old Larry Driscoll. But that had its compensation: Irv hadn't been able to sleep because of him.

Larry paid attention to Irv's every word. The more businesslike Irv became, the more remote his glance, the more critical his manner, the more Larry loved him.

"Your uncle's a *presence*," Esther whispered at the table. There were tears in her eyes. She had chosen Babe.

She put a motherly hand over Mandy's. "So tell me, how is my favorite author doing?"

But there was a tinge of reserve, because she already knew and because of the deeper suspicion that she no longer entertained.

"The hell with me. How are you doing, Esther?" he asked with feeling, Babe in front of his eyes.

"I don't complain."

Mandy thought, how old she is. It was as if she had taken one long leap over passing time; now she waited patiently for time to catch up. When it did, there would be no surprise for her, as there would be for Mandy, who — all men are boys — still played at the game of life.

"I thought you would have found a fellah by now."

"She has," Suzanne answered. "Barry Gray."

"Don't you be so smart, young lady!" Esther snapped. "Her uncle spoils her, as you can see. I keep up."

Larry and Irv came over. "Hello, Esther," Larry said. "Good to see you. Did you have a comfortable trip?"

"A trip's a trip. And how are you? You're looking swell."

"Just fine, thank you. And you, Suzanne. Haven't seen you in a while. How are you doing?"

"What's it to you?"

"Suzanne!" her mother admonished. "Larry's only being polite."

"Larry is always *only* being polite," she said bitingly, turning away from him.

The smile froze on Larry's face. "I seem to be in the minority, that's for sure."

He looked at Mandy. "Should I book you through the next week?"

"Of course," Irv answered for him. "Just figure Mandy's here till he says otherwise."

"Sure," Suzanne said. "Mandy's a good baby sitter. The best! Keep him here!"

She looked at her mother's bristling, worried face. At her uncle's non-committal and remote stare. At Larry, the sweet-smiling bastard. She couldn't catch Mandy's eye. She felt everyone at the table — flesh of her flesh, flesh on her flesh — stifling her. Perhaps it was the lack of sleep combined with her period that allowed her irritation to overcome her. "Damn you all!" she said. Got up. Her chair fell over behind her. She rushed out.

"Oh, shit!" said Mandy in resignation, standing up. He followed after her.

"Nice. A very nice family reunion," said Esther. "In front of the whole world."

Irv didn't answer.

Larry walked away — with an idea of what Mandy was chasing.

⚜ ⚜ ⚜

Esther was a good judge of character. While she was humoring this one and that with a "yes," she took notice. But the McCarthy days as well as her own proclivities had taught her truth was not to be taken outside the family.

Even so, the next day, she confided in Larry.

She had taken a walk by herself in the afternoon along the top of the hill, way past the dining hall and the girls' tennis courts to the girls' basketball court.

She found Larry by himself. She sat on an enameled chair and watched him dribble the ball and hook baskets. The court was shaded by a high wall.

He had a fine body, almost hairless except for the sparse strands under his arms. The flush of activity gave his white skin the clotted tones of peaches under sour cream. She could guess at his jockstrap under his silk trunks. She wondered if he were circumcised — a lot of gentiles were.

But still.

To even *think* of getting involved with a goy.

Maybe she didn't know her own daughter.

She herself couldn't imagine.

He dribbled and shot, dribbled and shot, worked up quite a sweat before he acknowledged seeing her.

"Hi!" he called and came over. Took up the sweatshirt from the chair next to her, put it over his shoulders and sat down.

"Whew! Want an orange?" he asked, pointing to the bag at his feet.

"No," she answered but reached for the bag to hand him.

"That one looks nice," she said as he peeled one.

The air was full of the smell of orange and clean sweat.

"How's your daughter today? Still damning all of us?"

"Oh, don't take her seriously. She was just under the weather."

"Mandy was a real hero to go after her. Did he survive?"

"Haven't you seen him?"

"I wash my hands of famous authors, temperamental kids, and even the almighty Uncle himself. The whole Bender clan, except you, Esther. You don't cause waves."

"Oh, come on now." But she was gratified.

"Anyway, this is the first day off *I've* taken all summer. Let them look for me if they need me. Let Mandy keep Irv company."

"You don't like Mandy, do you?"

"He's a pain in the ass."

His one-of-the-boys language pleased her. She knew the world. "Well, Irv will just have to make his peace, that's all. You see, if he were a man to go back on his word, it would be different. But in the long run, no matter how he talks, he's not. If Mandy decides to be a real butt-inski and come back in, what can Irv do? Of course business is business. Am I talking out of turn?" Esther asked, noticing the cold set to Larry's eyes.

"I haven't been told Mandy wants back in," Larry said.

"Neither have I! Don't get me wrong. Irv hasn't said a word. But I have eyes. I see. I knew Mandy from before I knew anything. So don't you be mad at Irv. He needs you now. He's got problems. He always keeps his aggravation to himself. He'll kill himself yet, taking everything on his own two shoulders. I hate to say it, but if I could talk, I'd tell him, don't take the world on your shoulders. What has Mandy done for you? You don't need him. Suzanne doesn't either. I don't like his effect on her. Between her professors and her uncle's friends she'll never get her feet on the ground."

"Am I one of her uncle's friends?"

Her voice changed. Her look took on significance. "I can never thank you enough," she whispered.

"Don't thank me, Esther. Anything could have happened, but nothing did."

"That's why I'm thanking you. Because I know nothing *will*. I'm a good judge of character. I keep my mouth shut, but I see what's going on around me. So I thank you from the bottom of a mother's heart."

Her mother's heart expanded, reached out to him. What if this Irish boy said to her, "Oh, mother Esther, you are so wise, let me lean on you"? The wedding night she had never had — when the flesh of the groom satiates every sacred desire — played tricks on her once more.

Then she controlled herself.

Thought positively.

Shooed away the devil — an adolescent girl.

And thanked Larry again for not deflowering her virgin. But this time her whisper was full of her own heart. The good judge of character reached out to a good boy.

"Mandy's changed," she said. "Gotten very selfish as he's gotten older. Three wives! Can you imagine? He can kid himself all he wants, but *that* won't make him any younger. He's a bad influence, I can feel it in my blood. Hollywood ruined him. Turned his head. You won't believe it, but he didn't know from women when he was younger. He and Irv were like this" (she crossed her fingers). "The future is what they thought about. But he grew silly as he grew older. Always looking at me so deeply. 'Esther, dear, how *are* you?' As if he cared. That's just the way he used to look at my late husband. Personally, I think he's nearsighted."

Larry laughed.

"Thank God someone around here has a sense of humor. One word to my daughter and she flies off the handle."

"Suzanne takes everything too seriously."

"Yes sir, that's my daughter."

"But she has all the advantages. She'll do okay."

"Don't you worry," said Esther, placating the bitterness in his voice. "A young man doesn't need what a girl has to have. *He* can make his own way. Like my brother-in-law did. So don't you envy others, you got plenty going for you." She patted his hand without a qualm. "Not least of all, Irv. He's not a man to tell you how he feels, to put things in words. But I can tell you for him — he counts on you. He has real feeling for you — like a younger brother. And I feel for you through him. You can count on me."

She smiled at him; she felt wonderful. She had come her own special distance away from an emotion.

"Maybe you're put out because Irv's spent all day with Mandy. But he has to spend some time with him. He's in a bind. Well, there's nothing I can do. After dinner, I go back to the real world. But why don't you please him? Come have dinner with us. Surprise him. Take a meal at the Oak Room!"

"I don't know…"

"Come on," she coaxed. "Suzanne's eating with the camp. Come keep me company."

Larry shrugged. "Thank you, Esther. Another time. Mandy's done nothing but snub me since he's come. I don't have to sit down to eat with him."

"You shouldn't take things so personally! I'm sure Mandy means no harm. He's just absent-minded, always was. You should have more confidence in yourself."

He was quiet, looked out over the hills. She didn't like him brooding. "But don't let me interrupt your game. I'll sit here and watch."

He got up. Folded his sweatshirt and put it on the chair.

He went back to his game. She left soon after. She didn't want to make him self-conscious while he played.

⚜ ⚜ ⚜

Larry walked in on Suzanne after taps. She was sitting on her bed reading. Expecting Mandy later on.

"Why, Larry!"

"Aren't you going to invite me to lie down?"

She blushed. "It's too late for that." What a thing to say! Her regretful tone embarrassed her even more.

"You only do it with one at a time, hah?"

"Don't talk to me like that!"

"Oh! Oh!" His hands flew back. He looked at her contemptuously and flexed his face into short, quick grimaces of mock horror. "Forgive me, princess. I forgot you shit ice cream."

She put down her book. "I never said I shit ice cream." Then the absurdity of the retort made her giggle. "See how you make me act!"

"I saw yesterday. You made a fool of me in front of your family and your boyfriend. You two setting a date yet?"

"What are you talking about?"

"You and Mandy."

"I don't know what you mean." She was a feeble liar and would have told him the truth, if he hadn't been in such a dangerous mood. "But I *am* sorry, Larry, and I apologize for what I said yesterday. I didn't want to bother you anymore or else I'd have come and told you so."

"All of a sudden it matters to you if you bother me!"

"I *said* I'm sorry."

"What does it matter if you're sorry? You did it, didn't you?"

"I *said* I apologize."

"That'll get you time off with good behavior!"

"Oh," she moaned. She was very vulnerable to the secret of his early life. Now she hated herself.

"Christ, don't cry!"

"It's my period. It turns me inside out."

"Oh, is that what you meant about it being too late? You didn't mean you were going to bed with Mandy, you meant you had your period. Is that it?" He sat down next to her and with mocking lovingness put his arm around her. "How about a kiss, then?"

"No."

"Why not? What's to stop you? Your period?" She looked into his burning eyes and saw him suffering.

"Forgive me, Larry. Forgive me. All right?"

"Come on, just a little kiss."

"Not like this."

"How then?"

He came closer to her. "How then?" he whispered.

He didn't want her tongue in his mouth, the hushed smell of her blood encircling them. But he traced her face with his finger. She looked at him imploringly. Then she kissed him passionately.

"You've wanted this for a long time," he said in the same melodic whisper. "Tell me how."

She unzipped his fly and put her hand on his cock.

"Not that way, princess," he said languidly, and then reached up into her long red hair, made a fist of it, and pulled her down.

When he came there wasn't much, but she hadn't learned to swallow. He saw the mess on his pants. "Damn it!" he said, turning from it, and then from her when he saw her staring at him hungrily, her lips and chin wet.

He got up and went to the toilet.

He took his time.

When he came out he was freshly combed and there were water spots on his fly. "You'd better get washed," he said.

"Is that all you have to say?"

"What do you want? A poem about a blow job?"

"Why are you treating me like this?"

"Act like a cunt, you'll be treated like one."

He had gone too far, and realized it when he saw the pain on her face. He'd end up with a basket case on his hands. They'd all blame him. He had no luck.

"Ah, come on, Suzanne. Be a sport. Give us a smile, Suzanne. I'm sorry. Give us a smile."

She only closed her mouth. He left her there, staring red-eyed into space.

❧   ❧   ❧

Irv had been reading too. Or holding a book. It was after midnight. His eyes were strained. He didn't know what he was going to do.

Or, more accurately, he didn't know how he was going to do it. He had sat there with Mandy earlier and had not done it.

Mandy had brought back the past. Not the chimera of nostalgia that appeared in Mandy's eyes. The concrete past. What had been and would be no more.

What had been.

And what had been had *really* been.

Was as real as the present.

But had passed.

Babe had been Babe.

Mandy had been Mandy.

Larry would be Larry.

There was no stopping it. We are what we are. And — being back with Mandy again, threw it in his face — we are what we were. In Irv's business, even he was forced to look at baby pictures sometimes.

Big heads on small bodies, while the parents coo.

Where the hell had Larry disappeared to? Irv was ready to go out and search for him, when he walked in.

"Where the hell have you been all day?"

"Finding out the truth."

"About what?"

"About everything."

"Tell me the truth about everything. I have all night."

"You tell *me!*"

"I don't know the truth about everything."

"Well, start with Mandy cutting back into the camp."

"Who told you that?"

"A big bird."

"Now you sit down. That's right, sit. How many times do I have to tell you. Come to me! Speak your mind!"

"You speak yours! You say you love me and all the time you're thinking of cutting your old partner back in."

"I'll take care of Mandy. I handle my own business."

"You want to handle your niece's too? She and Mandy are sleeping together."

"What?"

"I knew yesterday at lunch when he ran after her like a lap dog. And I went to make sure tonight. Mandy's taught her a hell of a lot in a short time. I can vouch for that."

Irv was silent. Mandy do a think like that? Mandy? Mandy was Mandy. Why he'd trust him with — what? And Suzanne? Women. He'd had enough of women's problems. His mother all his life. Esther's hysterectomy. Let Esther take care of this. Let mother and daughter work out this mystery together.

His father made a rare appearance in his mind. Solly Bender walked ahead of his wife, a flask in his pocket.

Solly always offered his older son a snort. "Best medicine." The big little boy always refused because of the mother in his heart.

"Solly!" she'd shriek when she saw him up to that trick.

"Shut up, kvetsh. Better than mother's milk," Solly would whisper to his six-year-old.

A lifetime of hate lifted out of Irv's heart.

Mandy barged in.

"You fucking punk," he said, grabbing Larry by his clean shirt and punching him.

Solly Bender and Mandy berserk sent Irv back to mean poverty, to Yiddish accents, to the house on Stegman Parkway.

"Fight, God damn you, fight!" Mandy yelled, shaking him.

But Larry had the mentality of an ex-con. Accused of a bungled crime, he pleaded innocent. He hadn't done anything. He wasn't going to resist arrest. He played it smart. "Damn you!" Mandy yelled and pushed him off. "You fool!" he said, turning to Irv. "He's no good! For God's sake, throw him out of here!"

"You okay?" Irv whispered to Larry. He stood up, walked over to him. "Are you sure you're okay?" Larry's cheeks were striped red and Irv was mad with concern.

"I'm okay."

"He's messing up Suzanne," Mandy yelled.

"Go to the bathroom, Larry. Take care of yourself. I'll be right there. I want to speak with Mandy first."

"About what? About me? Don't listen to him!"

"Don't give orders!"

"He'll lie."

"It doesn't matter if he tells the truth," Irv said. "Nothing matters between us. When will you understand?"

"It'll matter," said Mandy after Larry left the room. "What I'm going to tell you will matter."

Irv sat down. "Then in that case I don't want to hear."

"You're gonna hear."

"Mandy, pack and get out of here."

"Just like that?"

"Just like that."

"And the camp?"

"You were paid for your share."

"Peanuts."

"You got what you asked for."

"And your promise?"

"Show it to me."

"So that's it. You know, I don't care. I don't give a shit about the money. You can take your fucking camp and shove it! But Suzanne! That bastard is hurting her. He's making her suffer. I won't sit by!"

"From what I hear, you haven't been sitting by. There was no trouble here before you came. There will be no trouble after you leave. I'll see to that. You brought trouble with you, now take it back to where you belong."

"Don't you care about Suzanne?"

"She's my niece. And if *you* care about her, you'll leave like a man."

"Larry's —"

"There's nothing I want to hear."

They sat in silence for a long time, as if to test Irv's words. Mandy had made it easy for Irv. For all along he had unconsciously expected the worst.

"Where am I going to go?" Mandy asked himself softly. "Suzanne needs me, believe me about that, Irv. And I gotta get some money somewhere."

"I'll lend you five thousand against your new book."

"Five thousand? What the hell can I do with five thousand?"

"You saying no?"

Mandy looked around wildly. All of this had been his idea. Without him, without his money, without his imagination Irv wouldn't be sitting where he was. And the bastard must know it, thought Mandy, calm now that the worst had happened, crafty now that he had nothing. Nothing. It made him feel good. He looked right into Irv's eyes and revived. "I'm saying lend me ten."

⚜ ⚜ ⚜

The next day Mandy slept late. He left his room in the early afternoon and began to walk. When he got to the girls' side, rather than continuing on to Suzanne, he went toward Sugar Loaf, "the rolling hill" of the girls' alma mater song. Though it bordered the girls' side it was off limits to the campers. He was in better shape than when he was younger, and easily strolled up it, avoiding the soft cow dung as he went.

He didn't think things out. He never knew what he'd do until he did it, what he'd write till he wrote it. In a sense he always carried his baggage with him. He tucked his big mistakes into small corners and hoped they'd get lost.

He sat near the top of the hill and looked over the girls' side. He could see way up to the mess hall and to Irv's house. The bedroom where Irv and Larry spent the night...

What a view of Camp Rose Lake. The wide vista of his idea paying off for someone else.

Anyone can make a mistake.

Forget it. Things would work themselves out. They'd have to.

Suzanne's ignorance was none of his business. Abel was none of Cain's business. After the fact.

Ah, shit! Go know.

Then he was distracted.

He heard footsteps behind him and turned to see two young campers coming from the other side of the hill. Since Sugar Loaf was off limits, the girls often snuck up for a smoke.

These two still held their lit cigarettes.

"What are you girls up to?" he asked. He had only said the first thing that came to him. After all, who were they to him? Yet his voice sounded threatening even to him and the dark, pubescently pudgy girl dropped her cigarette, which touched her bare leg as it fell. She stamped it out. The girl had a round face and oily skin. She was terribly frightened at being caught and at the same time angry at herself, as if she had marred a perfect record. She suddenly began to giggle.

The other girl motioned as if to drop her cigarette and then, instead, flicked her ash.

"What are you trying to do? Burn down the place?" Mandy growled at her.

She was the taller of the two and had lightish hair, a rather large nose, and clear skin. She wore glasses with blond rims that blended with her complexion and made her appear quite plain. She was about thirteen, like her friend, but more anonymous. Only her defiance made her stand out.

Deliberately, she took a drag. Only then, slowly, did she drop her cigarette and snuff it out.

"Ya sure it's out?"

"Positive," she mouthed slowly.

"Wipe that smirk off your face."

He hated the girl's arrogance.

"What's your name?" he demanded.

She didn't answer.

"Don't report us, mister," the pudgy one begged and again giggled.

"Your friend here deserves a good lesson," he said pointing at the blondish girl. "Smoking at your age!" His hand was shaking.

The defiant girl looked straight at him. Her actions seemed to be surprising her as much as they were enraging him.

"Rena's not like this, really she's not!"

Neither was Mandy, who cried, "Rena, is it!"

"That's right!" Rena brazened it out. "So what?"

"So you better watch your step, young lady, that's what!" Mandy stood up.

Rena stared, and then lifted her hands between them and blurted, "You're not my father! You can't scare me!"

She looked at him for one more moment, then shrugged her shoulders, walked right past him, and started down the hill.

"Can I go too?" the pudgy one asked. "Please."

"What's stopping you?"

She hesitated, then said, "Thanks," and ran like hell after her friend. After a while he heard her giggles, derisive and spiteful as she ran.

My God, he thought to himself. What's gotten into me? His mouth tasted dirty, as if his tongue had touched an old penny. He was tarnished and alone.

⚜   ⚜   ⚜

But while Mandy was on the mountain, he received a week's reprieve. There was a fire in the kitchen. Irv began to bat it down when some shmegegge threw water on the oil blaze. Irv's arm was badly burned.

The accident was an omen.

Afterward, a lot of people said it never rains but it pours. And things happen in threes.

But for Mandy the omen held hope. Not that he wished Irv a right arm in a sling. Or the pain of burning. No, but it gave him an edge. It gave him time for Suzanne and himself. Larry literally became attached to Irv, and Irv, in the infirmary, was far away.

Larry had done Suzanne sexual damage, obliterated her ego, sent her into a trauma of self-doubt, into spasms of guilt. She saw herself as some sort of monster. A nymphomaniac. A cunt.

Mandy would never forget walking into the shack and finding her. It took days before she let him make love to her again, after a long, long talk.

When the time came for him to leave, they went to the Point L House for dinner — to be by themselves. But there was square-dancing that evening and the place was jammed. Joan Anna and her husband and a grown daughter were there and Mandy and Suzanne went over to say hello. The owner found a table for them in the meantime and they were trapped.

They ordered their dinner as the caller stepped onto his box in front of the country musicians. The music started up. The caller began his twang and the farmers and their wives stamped along the wooden floor. Thin, weather-beaten men, buxom wives in homemade skirts. Many many faces that had passed through the camp over the years.

Joan Anna seemed reluctant to dance, but her husband insisted, so she shrugged in the direction of Mandy and Suzanne, got up and joined a set.

The daughter went with the younger dancers. The girls looked sluttish because of their colorful attempts at high fashion, the young men too respectable in their shiny suits. Many in this group still worked at the camp, on the grounds, in the laundry, in the kitchen. They were Suzanne's age. They danced in the same room but in a different world.

What world did she belong to? She felt lost, especially now that Mandy was really going away. He had decided to go back to Italy. Where else would ten grand take him? He told her that he had lost the world, and now he was ready to gain himself. And he didn't say a word against her uncle.

They were both planners. Next summer she'd go to Italy. He'd show her everything. At the table they discussed what was going to be. In the fervor of the future and the music, they began to enjoy themselves.

"Hey," said Mandy, "we walked into a good night after all!"

After the first set, the caller stepped away and went back to his beer. Their steaks arrived and they ate.

The band struck up a polka and the Polish farmers got up to dance. There was a moment of excitement, as there can be anywhere in America when a minority suddenly seizes on its past. The music got faster and faster, the dancers spun around. Verve was all, though the steps seemed perfectly executed to Suzanne and Mandy, who had no idea of how much had been lost.

"Hey, let's dance!" he said.

She laughed. In all these years, camp people had never danced at the Point L House.

"Come on," he said and stood up. He meant it. For a moment she was offended. Then she looked up at him, vulnerable, tender, waiting to dance with the Poles.

"Damn it, why not?" she said and got up too.

People from the camp, country people. Jews, Poles, hicks. The owner's niece, the rest of the world. Mandy Mershheimer, anybody. He mixed things up.

Suddenly she loved him for it.

They swung around the floor, keeping a beat, going faster and faster.

They caused quite a stir.

The dance didn't end, it slowed down, trailed off into an ambiguous love song. Young people grabbed each other close.

Mandy, with no shame at all, danced with both arms around her waist. The room darkened, she smelled lilies of the valley, felt the skirts made stiff by crinolines touch her pants-covered legs.

She closed her eyes; gave Mandy the lead.

"I love you," he whispered in her ear.

"You wouldn't say that if you weren't going away tomorrow."

"You're too smart," he complained. "But stay that way."

"Take me with you."

"I love you too much for that. Next summer, baby. Next summer."

"I'll be lost without you."

"Not if you dance when the music plays."

"Let's go now."

"Before we have our cantaloupe and ice cream?"

"Yes."

"Okay, but you're twisting my arm."

When the music stopped, he went over to say good-bye to Joan Anna. Suzanne waved and then waited on the porch, listening to the August rain. Mandy came out and ran through the rain to the car. When he picked her up, his face was still wet.

❧ ❧ ❧

He left the next morning. Larry drove him. All very civilized. Irv, arm in sling, shook hands with him southpaw. Suzanne kissed him on the cheek. She spoke to Larry. In a matter of fact way she told him to drive carefully, in order to show Mandy she could make it on her own.

When they drove off, and it was her only inkling (if that's what it was), she felt extremely tired and depressed. When her uncle said he didn't need any help, she went off by herself, though he would have rather had her stay.

In the car, Mandy thought he'd say something to Larry. But he kept still. Larry, uneasy, waited for the words that didn't come. And in the meantime drove like Irv.

Nothing happened between them.

Except they were uncomfortable.

And the roads were wet.

The car skidded. Larry lost control for an instant and crashed into a telephone pole.

When Mandy opened his eyes everything was very quiet. A camera had landed on the front seat.

Mandy decided Irv would want it back.

So he got out of the car and walked back along the road. It was very foggy and the heavy early morning moisture was chilly. He kept pace to the poem in his head.

Bells! Bells! Bells!

The tintinnabulation that so musically wells from the bells, bells, bells,

Bells, bells, bells, bells...

He chanted out loud as he walked, "Oh, the jingling and the tinkling of the bells, bells, bells."

A horn shattered the swinging and the ringing, the rhyming and the chiming of the bells.

"What you up to, mister?"

"Me?" Mandy felt the bump on his head. "Returning a camera to Irving Bender."

"Camp Rose Lake?"

"Keeping time, time, time, in a sort of runic rhyme," Mandy answered.

"Get in!"

But Mandy leaped like a dancer onto the back of the truck. The farmer started up and Mandy hummed with the jingling and the wrangling, the sinking and the swelling, the clamor and the clangor of the bells, bells, bells, bells, bells...

Irv was dozing on the couch when the front door slammed open.

Mandy limped in (he had sprained his ankle jumping off the truck).

His clothes were torn and muddy.

Blood was caked on the side of his face.

His left arm hung limply at his side. In his right hand he held Irv's camera without its case.

Irv was confused at first. This couldn't be Mandy. The apparition was the result of the pills he had been taking for his pain.

"You shouldn't be so careless, leaving your camera lying around."

It was Mandy. The same old Mandy. He had walked right in, a big expectant grin on his swollen face.

"There," said Mandy, throwing the camera on the couch next to Irv.

Mission accomplished, he collapsed. He cut open the other side of his head on Irv's coffee table as he fell.

Irv passed his left hand over Larry's face. "You're looking okay, considering." There was hardly a scratch on him.

"Did I total the Caddy?"

"I'll buy another. Two. One for you."

Larry smiled weakly. "That's it, reward incompetence."

"Accidents happen. Was it Mandy's fault?"

"I was driving. Where's Mandy?"

"At the infirmary at camp."

"You lying to me?"

"No, he's not, Larry," said Suzanne, who had had to drive her uncle to the hospital. She approached the bed.

"Hello, Suzanne. Nice of you —"

"Don't mention it."

"How's Mandy?"

"Okay, really. Okay. He's more banged up than you, that's all."

"How'd he get back to camp?"

"He walked and hitched. He'll be all right."

"Will I get another chance to drive him to the airport?"

"Not this season," Irv said. "Just you get well. Worry about yourself."

"I'm okay. Just weak."

"You rest."

"Okay."

He fell asleep.

Suzanne and Irv consulted with the doctor in his office. Larry had been taken to the Adventist Hospital in Carbondale. The doctor was a young-looking man with a permanent, well-meaning, impersonal smile on his face. He pointed to the X rays.

"... So, you see, it would be moving him unnecessarily. He might as well rest comfortably here."

"There's nothing left to do?" Irv repeated.

The doctor shook his head. "Call his next of kin. That's all."

Irv walked over to the X rays. Larry inside out and crushed to death. "How long?" Irv asked.

"Long enough to make arrangements. Maybe a day."

"Shouldn't he be told?" Suzanne cried out.

The doctor looked at Irv. His eyes said, "Women." Then he noticed the signs of pain on Irv's face. "Is that arm bothering you? He's not a relative of yours, is he, Mr. Bender?"

Irv shook his head. Walked out.

Suzanne went back to Larry alone.

"Hi," he said.

"Hi. We've just been with the doctor. Everything's okay. Uncle's too impatient. He's in the car already. He wants to get back to camp."

A look of joy came over Larry's face. "Now that he knows I'm all right, he's really pissed, isn't he? He never liked me to drive the Caddy. Always thought the camp car was better on these roads. He'll never let me live it down, I bet."

He made it easy for her to lie. "Well, he's not really angry, he's just got a lot to do with you away. And he only has one good arm to do it with."

"Do you know what last rites are?"

"Sure."

"When I woke up, that's what I found. A priest. He asked for my confession."

"He must have gotten an earful."

"You should know the half of it."

"Well, it looks like you won't be burning in hell for a little while longer," she said, her tone full of the old sarcasm.

She never saw a man so happy in her life.

On the way back to camp, Irv said, "Take me to Joan Anna's place."

"How is he?" Joan Anna asked. They all stood on the wet grass.

Suzanne shook her head.

"God help us," Joan Anna replied.

Irv walked past them into the house.

He stayed there through the ordeal. In the little wooden room where Mandy had finished his book.

Two days.

Sitting in a chair.

Staring out the window.

No one dared tell him what was good for him: sleep, clean clothes, fresh bandages, food, a shave. He was the boss. Joan Anna was in attendance.

Suzanne took care of all the arrangements. Visited Mandy. Visited Larry.

Death was the dirty little secret at Rose Lake. Kept to a whisper at the summer camp. Hushed up in the sickroom too.

Larry outlived the doctor's prognosis. On the second night his small room was crowded. He was in high spirits, full of dope. "Dance for me, Ralph," he asked the boys' nature counselor, a high-school teacher, a middle-aged vegetarian, who kept to himself. He had a spare body and skin as tan as bark. He jumped into a weird modern dance. Rhythmatics, it was called.

People moved back and clapped and hummed while Ralph danced.

Death advanced lovingly. Larry's white, white skin became translucent, his blue eyes blazed. And his smile held the promise of preparedness, as if his spirit knew.

Death was advancing like an angel when Larry's mother beat it to him.

Esther drove her up. Mrs. Driscoll was the epitome of gentility in the midst of strangers. When she said, "You people," she meant Jews, and when she exclaimed, "I knew that man was turning his head," she meant Irv had killed her son. Esther rued her own understanding of human nature and kept on driving.

She was a short fat woman, Mrs. Driscoll, with white hair and a cultured voice. Her maiden name was known in Jersey City. But she had made a bad marriage and God punished her by the wildness of her sons. She had three of them.

Larry was the rotten apple of her eye.

Suzanne brought her mother and Mrs. Driscoll to the hospital. By now Suzanne was on the side of the angels. Larry had given every sign that he did not want to know. Took Irv's absence to mean he wasn't badly hurt. Took his lack of sensation to mean he was resting. Took the euphoric effect of the dope to mean he was healing fine.

But Mrs. Driscoll broke down when she got to his room. All his life he had felt the burden of her love, now the burden was mixed with dread and horror.

Suzanne tried to move her from his side. But she leaned over him, wailing. When she gained control — he had turned to marble in her arms — she wiped her eyes and sat down.

"Of course you'll be all right," she said, dabbing a dainty white handkerchief to her eyes, her shiny white plastic pocketbook still on her arm and opened. "These people say you've seen a priest. But what a comfort it would be to me if —"

She stopped. His mouth had opened like an animal's. His eyes closed, his face twisted. He was screaming without making a sound.

"Where does it hurt?" his mother asked.

He died that night. The old Larry. Full of hostility, panic, and hate. A priest in attendance.

He was buried outside Scranton. The mourners came from the church and found Irv waiting by the open grave with Joan Anna. No one dared to approach him. Wretchedly haggard, expressionless, he could not control his tears with his left hand.

Mandy was on the opposite side of the grave by Suzanne and Esther. He was battered, but no worse for wear. Irv could see him through the blur: irony of ironies.

Mrs. Driscoll stayed close to the priest.

It was a beautiful day. Heavy white clouds glistened under the sun. The creak of the coffin being lowered, Mrs. Driscoll's sobs, and the Latin evocation rose in the clear air.

⚜ ⚜ ⚜

Suzanne drove to Joan Anna's that night to pick up her uncle.

Joan Anna echoed Mandy's words. "Don't expect too much."

She shrugged and knocked on the door to the guest room.

"Come in," he said.

He was sitting on the chair looking out the window. The black sky was full of small cold stars. She walked over to the windowsill and sat on it. Light came in through the opened door.

"Ready, Uncle?"

No response.

She didn't expect anything, only his love. So she sat with him, silently, for what seemed an endless night. He was as remote as the dark sky. His pain was more unalterable than hers. It nearly broke her heart.

"Uncle Irv," she whispered tremulously, "it's me, Suzanne."

And again, as he did not stir, "It's me, Uncle, it's me, Suzanne."

Irv looked at her. The bitterness in his eyes echoed in his words. "So what?"

PART THREE

Mandy Found Out he was a Jew in Israel in 1961 while on assignment with an Italian film crew. Suzanne, who had been living with him since Larry died, used the time alone in Rome to run away. He never understood why she hadn't talked things over with him first. In Tel Aviv he got a letter postmarked Jersey City begging him to forgive her. He wrote back he understood.

He stayed on. Put himself into his people, his people into the heart of history, re-examined the causes of the Second World War, and wrote *The Promise*. His damaged soul and his lined face conspired in a sentimental vision of history. He spent two years getting his facts straight. Then over them he placed the cataract of his feelings.

The Promise became a best seller in America. The sale of the paperback rights set a record. The musical threatened never to close on Broadway. The film was shot on location and won awards. Mandy returned home a hero.

Americans loved *The Promise*. You didn't have to be Jewish to agree that something of great value had been lost. Exactly *what*, Mandy never resolved. But once values had been better, families closer, people stronger, life harder and more meaningful. Less was more.

He believed everything he wrote in *The Promise*. Its rewards became his virtue. He shared that virtue on the talk shows, speaking with the authority of a renowned man on the verge of making a grand bequest. His arteries hardening, his hearing impaired, he became a raconteur.

He no longer dwelled on his wrinkles. Time had temporarily stopped for him. He thought he had mellowed into wisdom. But it was his success and the smiling people whose words he half heard that made a case for his immortality. And for the soundness of his opinions. Politically he had been a liberal; as his ideas became more conservative he called them liberal too.

Listen, he wasn't Barry Goldwater. He didn't wear suits. Rather, expensive dungarees. Batik shirts. He allowed his hair to grow out gray and kinky and wore it in a natural cut. He believed in legalizing pot, abortion, and in what he quaintly called sexual expression. After all, you don't become the darling of the talk shows if you're a zombie.

In more serious interviews, he was convinced Nixon was Israel's true friend, so he supported him on Vietnam. He hadn't voted for him in '68, but he would in '72.

On late-nite TV Mandy pontificated and beamed like a baby. Then he moved one seat over, Ed McMahon sold dog food, and Johnny Carson, dressed like everyone's dentist, led the next self-promoter down the path of banality.

Self-promoter? Mandy wouldn't argue. He had learned to do business like an American. But in his personal relationships he thought only of others. His soul took on the structure of an organized charity. He concentrated on the good he intended to do and ignored the seventy percent he pocketed for expenses.

So on that balmy March day in 1970 he had a good reason for calling Suzanne and telling her to meet him in Miami. Irv needed her. But he didn't wait for her outside the Fontainebleau as he had promised. "Damn him!" Suzanne cursed before she got out of her rented car. She had told him to be outside. She knew he wouldn't be.

She was dressed in blue, jeans and a sleeveless jersey that emphasized her ample breasts and her slim and competent arms. Her thinner face revealed not so much the passing of the years as their strain. She had the taut, neurotic intensity about the eyes that one sees everywhere. When she smoked dope she giggled, and came down quick.

She looked for Mandy in the lobby, then phoned him, and finally went to his room.

"Sweetheart!" Mandy called as he opened the door. Then he looked around. "Didn't your boyfriend come down too?" he asked in mock alarm. She had threatened he would.

"No, my *friend's* not coming."

He kissed her. She gave him a quick, dismissive hug.

"Come in, Suzanne. I'm just about ready. You *are* looking beautiful. Your boyfriend must be doing something right."

"His name is Jim."

"Oh, I know his name."

"And he's my *friend.*"

"Who says he isn't?"

Mandy pointed to the couch. "Let's sit for a minute and catch up. We've got time."

"Do we?" she asked. But she sat. They hadn't seen each other since she had photographed his wife for *Ms.*, eight months ago. This one was a Greek aristocrat opening a chain of boutiques. "So, how have you been, Mandy?"

"I can't complain," he said in a way that made them think of Irv. He put his hand to his wiry hair, which mushroomed over his old man's thin, denim-clad body. "Funny, me being here when Irv gets sick. All these years I wanted to make peace with that guy."

Irv had never forgiven Mandy for taking his niece along with his money. But Mandy's conscience was clear. He had saved Suzanne in 1959. If he hadn't let her come to Rome with him, she would have ended up like Babe. He saw it in her eyes.

"...And then I find out he's right here at Cedars of Lebanon. So I walk into his hospital room with a bunch of flowers and sit down.

'Mandy,' he says.

'Who else?' I say.

I swear there were tears in his eyes."

"Don't exaggerate."

"I swear. Real tears. Me too."

"Mandy, Irv has spent the winters here for years and you know it."

"Sure I know. But how often do I get here? This place gives me the creeps. What was it John Ciardi said — the weather's fine once you realize you're dead. But the senior citizens come to hear me talk. I'm selling out the thirteenth paperback edition of *The Promise.* How do you like that?"

"Are you working on anything new?"

She was unimpressed. Her questioning annoyed him. She had no right to start. "I just signed to do a kids' book on the Passover service. Snooky is going to do the woodcuts. We're going to dedicate the book to your Beatrice (he used the Italian inflection). Do you think she'll like that?"

"It will be as close to religion as she has ever come."

"That's exactly the market these guys figure we're going to hit. We'll have the parents buying the book for themselves. You wait and see."

She smiled at his enthusiasm and she shrugged off his success. She had changed after she'd divorced her doctor. Analyzed, out for herself. He regretted the difference.

Looking at her, her red hair short and tangled to approximate an Afro, her face slightly flushed (it was a test being in a hotel room with him after avoiding him for months), he felt love at the discomfort below her sharp voice. He thrilled at riding out the storm of her experiences, waiting for them to take him farther in the end. It made him young.

He remembered the long talks in Italy, the week in Greenwich Village after he had returned to America and found her shattered and alone. He remembered every push he had given her as she picked up the pieces and made a new start. He would have gone to her goddamned wedding, if it wouldn't have made Irv stay away. Most of all, through the years, he remembered the long, long telephone conversations that they had placed to each other at any time from any place. When he paid his share of those extraordinary bills, it was almost like having sex with her.

"What's going on between you and your friend Jim?" he asked. "Does he make you happy?"

"Let's not talk about it, all right?"

"Oh, now we've got things we talk about and things we don't."

"Finally," she said calmly, but her eyes were trying to escape.

"I never get you at home when I call. How come?"

"That's none of your business."

"But I make it mine. For the last six months I've been running up phone bills talking with your kid or your mother. Where are you?"

She didn't answer.

"You leave your kid with Esther and sleep out with a guy whose unlisted number she's 'not allowed' to give me. What's going on?"

"I don't want you calling me at Jim's. Neither does he. This is none of your business."

"I told you, I make it mine. Your first concern should be Beatrice. That's what's wrong with this whole goddamn country. We have all the wrong priorities."

"Oh, Mandy, you and my mother must be hitting it off nowadays. Don't you worry about Beatrice. Let her father and me take care of her, all right?"

"She'll end up a poor little rich girl like you!"

Suzanne blushed fiercely. "Don't make prophecies! Beatrice is doing just fine. She has an extended family. Her father and his new wife, two new grandparents, a stepbrother, my mother, Jim, me. She's the lucky one."

"She has an uncle too."

"Did I ever fault what you do for her?"

Mandy looked surprised. "I meant Irv."

"Didn't I mention him? She has an uncle too."

❈ ❈ ❈

Irv sat at the pool of his condominium under a beach umbrella, a dog at his feet. He had bought the golden cocker spaniel to please a young man and in the end got stuck with him. The dog looked up at Irv with big sad eyes. He had been boarded while Irv was in the hospital and the regimentation had temporarily subdued him. Usually he was fussy and caused Irv grief.

"What's with you?" Irv asked.

The dog opened its mouth wide and whined.

"You'll be back to normal soon," said Irv, who wouldn't be. Taking the dog on its morning walk had exhausted him. Why not? A bad dream had woken him before dawn. "That's it!" he had said out loud in recognition.

"Yes, that's it," he said now to the dog. Then he looked at the empty pool. It was still early. Not that the pool ever got much use.

Irv was altered. His illness or discomfort or whatever, for the doctors at Cedars of Lebanon had not diagnosed it, had caused him to lose weight over the last couple of years. Everyone complimented him on how good he looked, so he pretended he had been on a diet. If he really wanted a diagnosis he'd leave Miami for Boston or New York. But what were specialists good for except sending him bills? He knew something was wrong. That was enough for him. Something can be wrong for a long, long time.

He wore a thick, wavy brown hair piece that covered the pasty, wrinkled skin of his skull and which brought one's eyes away from his chicken neck. He wore bright clothes (now that he was thinner) for distraction. And he had a deep tan, having learned to take sun like manna — that is, when it didn't make him dizzy, as it did today. He looked like everyone else. Death or nature or fate was playing with him, fitting him into the common mold before finishing him off.

After Larry there had been bars and beauty and young men he had tried to help. No love lasted. His generosity always turned against him. The confusion or vulnerability in the eyes of beauty always turned to hate. The abstract cynicism that once had power to protect Irv soured. And in last night's dream it had turned to truth.

Of course he was anxious about today. Mandy had suggested that Suzanne come down. At first Irv said no. But Mandy had not lost his gift of conviction. He knew in his heart that Suzanne would want to help out.

Maybe she really did want to see her uncle. Maybe Mandy did know something this time. That was the impression he gave.

Irv couldn't afford to offend Suzanne. They had become so distant that there'd been time for it to dawn slowly on Irv that she felt he was to blame. After she ran away he assumed that it was shame that made her address the letters that finally arrived to Esther only. But when she returned her attitude was clear. She treated him with the cold indifference with which she greeted half of Jersey City when it knowingly and maliciously greeted her, pretending to accept her mother's story that she'd been at school abroad.

She couldn't stay in town. Any more than Irv could live his life in Jersey now. She moved to New York. People bumped into her. People talked.

She did not return to Barnard. To Irv that meant she was lost.

He himself walked up the five flights to the hole in the Village she paid too much for to implore her with reason. When she understood the gist of his visit the expression on her face changed from tense expectation to derision. He couldn't stand the mess around him and left.

In those days her tangled hair was long, her pale skin was smudged, and when spring came she walked barefoot through the Village. In the park she picked up men.

This period was what Esther later referred to as the stage she went through. For Esther it ended when Mandy came home victorious and had a long talk with her. After that she got interested in photography and right away married a doctor in her class. Too good to be true, said Esther, who proved right. Four years, a career, a kid, but she didn't *love* him. Absurd. After that you didn't ask questions. A grown woman — you try not to see.

Now you had to see. Over the phone from New York she apologized for not bringing her boyfriend to sleep with her under her uncle's roof. Jim was allergic to dogs.

But it hadn't ended with Mandy's sage advice, as Esther thought. In the hospital, as Mandy autographed menus and temperature charts for the nurses, he told Irv it had ended with a badly botched abortion and months of self-hate and pain. Mandy's careless words confirmed Irv's worst suspicions. Mandy must have told his niece the truth about Larry and him years ago.

By now Suzanne would have guessed herself. But thirty is not an impressionable age. Irv, by the pool, felt once more a rankling bitterness for the performing fool who had betrayed him.

On many a sleepless night he had watched Mandy's orange face through the radiating darkness, smiling at the whole world. Imposter. Here was the man who had precipitated Larry's death. Here was the man who had torn away his last piece of flesh, who had ruined her, and then had written his best book. Irv liked *The Promise* a lot.

He had been right not to speak to him all these years. Whenever he felt anger at everything that had not worked out for him, he could express it by pointing a finger. But Irv had another self, sicker, paler, and bald, that was now for no one's eyes but his own. Mandy butted in on it at the hospital and thought he should call Suzanne. So he'd be here again today. Irv's guest.

Irv had given his niece everything. And she had made him pay for it. When she became interested in photography, he stocked her darkroom, slowly, carefully, below list. She'd open a box and thank him. The tone of her voice said this isn't it at all. This costs, he reminded her once. Her look reminded him he could pay.

But she had done something with her photography. She was rich enough not to suffer from the frustrations of freelancing, and she knew enough people to get a start. When the woman's movement came along she was there, and became established. It's my insides they are all talking about, she once said to him. Suzanne Schwartz Bender had a name.

"Schwartz?" Esther had asked, less than delighted. "Why drag that up again?"

Her name enticed Irv, made him realize the extent of his loss. She did not paint anymore. To any mention of her old water colors she responded, my embroidery you mean? He did not consider photography the same thing. Yet she was almost in his magic circle. All by herself she had a name.

If he had had a son —

He would have had a very weak son.

As it was, he had a niece who had found something more. Cut him out of it! And undervalued its worth. She was careless. She was arrogant. What she wanted was more of herself.

When he offered her advice, her eyes denied him. Her ridicule recalled not his mother, but Babe. It suggested they shared some nuance of the joke. It taunted him with recognition.

It made him want to reach her beyond the very set limits of themselves. It made him want to shout, Look! I did for you! If you're someone, it's because I am someone too!

What did it matter? The pleasure of his lifetime had been ordering good clothes for weak men. Of dressing up beauty so it looked strong. He thought he had known nothing of pleasure when he was young. But he too had been the same person his whole life through. He saw what he saw and if he liked it he believed there was more. So he tampered with it for its own good, improved it, ruined it. Till it came to nothing at all.

At his worst he was ruthless, blindly selfish, and cruel. At his best he was religious. Had there been a God he might have become devout. But he was just a religious man looking for something more. And a prosaic man — who believed, without ever stating it, that the more would include an explanation.

Had he had an imagination, he might have been a poet. Had he had an education, a professor. Just the same, he had had to look for more in a society that exalted the owners of things. Like the poets and the professors, he wasn't better than that society. He fit in. The thing is, he could have fit into others.

If the American dream ever lived on Stegman Parkway, it entered Irv's heart as an unacknowledged optimism about the mechanics of time. The minute hand goes round and round and round building up hours, days, months, years in linear progression.

He was sixty years old before he experienced (last night) the horrible certainty that time would suddenly stop short for him, *him* personally. The knowledge wouldn't cut into his habits. Like all the others like him in Miami, he'd go on with his routine. He'd walk the dog for exercise, sun himself, order new clothes, try to sleep at night. And in the summer he'd go north to take care of the business someone else was now managing for him. The camp wasn't what it had been, though there was an overflow of applicants who'd never know.

Unlike all the others, he hadn't had children to let him down. No one told him, look, you're as good as dead, why not give everything over to me now? Instead, he had a niece who was as much a stranger. More.

❧ ❧ ❧

At the side of the pool, Suzanne looked down on the rings Irv wore on his tanned fingers. They were exquisite. Her father's star sapphire had been taken off and given to her. To Beatrice. Whatever Irv gave her now, he offered up in the name of her little girl.

"How are you feeling now, Uncle Irv?" (Despite all the reasons for doing it, she still couldn't call him "Irv" to his face.) "Why didn't you let us know right away that you were ill?" she asked as Mandy brought over chairs.

Irv shrugged. "Doctors."

"Know nothings," Mandy said.

Suzanne looked around. "Are you alone?"

"I've got Bruce's dog here," he said pointing to the sleeping dog. He lift ed a hand and looked at Mandy. "Should I stay? Should I go home? Should I go to camp early? I'd just as soon stay here."

"Sure," Mandy answered heartily. "Where else can you get sun like this? Soak it up. By camp time you'll be good as new."

"Mother says she's ready to come down at a minute's notice —"

"I didn't want anyone at the hospital. I didn't want anyone here. Only Mandy doesn't wait for invitations and he's good at spreading the word."

Mandy smiled and patted his hand. "Irv —"

"Don't start. Don't try to soften me up. I've watched you tell Johnny Carson how to run the world and how to be rolfed. I think, this man took my money, my nineteen-year-old niece, then he writes a book like the Bible."

"Don't blame Mandy!"

"Who should I blame? You? We sheltered you. We should blame ourselves."

"If the shoe fits," Suzanne said with a shrug.

"Suzanne," Mandy said, "have mercy!"

"Mercy? I'm not that sick," Irv answered.

"Uncle Irv, let's not wander." There was the nervous tug at her eyes. Her tone reflected an impatience he had often secretly felt for his mother.

"We're here because we both want to help you. If you want to stay here, I think we should discuss it. You're feeling better now, but you're not superhuman. There's no reason in the world for you to recuperate all alone."

"Then why don't you and Beatrice come down here for the season and take care of me?" he mocked.

"No." She insisted on answering, "I have my own life to lead. We'll have to make other arrangements."

"I figured," Irv said slowly, "that you would be too busy to help out."

Suzanne walked over to the pool. Her uncle's invitation had been gratuitous — hadn't it? Surely he wouldn't want Beatrice here. He considered the child unruly and had developed toward her the surface irritability that led old men to talcum powder, witch hazel, Ben-Gay. He could not understand that Beatrice was her own person. She had not been made to conform to the adult world the way Suzanne had. Suzanne breathed deeply and returned, saying, irrelevantly, "I should have brought my bathing suit."

"You can't stand chlorine," Mandy reminded her. Anything he could tell her about herself excited him. He looked at her heavy breasts under the nylon. She made quite a statement when she didn't wear a bra.

Suzanne sat down. Rolled her wide-legged jeans past her knees, closed her eyes, and faced the sun.

"That sun's too strong for you," Mandy warned.

"Save your advice," Irv said.

"Uncle Irv," Suzanne said slowly after an interval. "What are you going to do?"

"Don't worry. I've been thinking. I spoke with Herb yesterday. He did a shopping for me."

"Who's Herb?" Mandy asked.

"No one salacious enough for you!" Suzanne remarked without meaning to. "Just an old school teacher Uncle knows."

Herb was a retired professor of biology from the old normal school in Jersey City. A pleasant man, soft and precise, who dressed for the beach in white and who gave the impression of having accrued some wisdom with his years. He had an old-fashioned Jewish sense of humor. He glanced at things sideways and made comments.

He had originally been forced to Miami because of his wife's health. She ached any place else. She must have been sicker than either of them believed, because she died. He did not leave. Comfort crept up on him, an old fellow traveler. "Watch out," he warned Irv when Irv began to think of buying his condominium. "There's nothing not to like here. Nothing positive. Nothing negative. If you're an optimist, it's plenty. If you're blind, it's paradise."

Herb's mother had been part of a Jewish emigrant family that had gone west. She had written a diary of her pioneering life, about her father's bungled attempts to build a roof that would keep out the rain, about her crazy aspirations. The diary was the magic of a semiliterate girl. The plans she made! She married a man who promised to take her back east. Back east he opened a nickelodeon and she had twins. The diary ended on that wry note, abruptly. Herb filled his days working on the manuscript — or meaning to. He talked with Irv about the editorial problems involved and read passages out loud. "Type it up, for God's sake. I'll have my niece send it to Mandel Mershheimer."

Suzanne listened to her uncle describe the manuscript to Mandy. "Tell him to send it to the Jewish Museum," said Mandy who was used to being asked for favors and had found his way of saying no. He kept his eyes on Suzanne.

"What did you and Herb talk about?" Suzanne asked. She came back into the shade.

"The idea of his moving in temporarily."

Suzanne nodded. "That's a good idea," she said soberly.

"The place is big enough. He'll help me out. I'll help him out. After all, what does he have?" Irv was referring to Herb's small pension and smaller apartment.

Irv looked at Mandy. "I don't want a nurse!"

"You'll be fine," Mandy said, looking at the pool.

"At camp I'll have all the help I need."

"Joan Anna still with you?"

Suzanne and Irv looked at him as if the question were tactless and unkind. "At camp I have all the help I need," he repeated. "Here I'll have Herb."

"And in Jersey you have mother, and I can always be reached if you really want me."

"Thank you," Irv said to his niece, formally but without malice.

"I'm going to go up now. This your key? I'll unpack."

"Take him," Irv said. She grabbed her overnight bag, took the leash, and ran with the dog.

⚜ ⚜ ⚜

Suzanne brought the dog into the darkened, carpeted, air-conditioned foyer, past the widow behind the reception desk, past the bleached-blue fountain with the putto on a rock, and on to the elevator that droned a melody like cellophane crackling. Her nipples tightened in the cold and she looked at herself in the gilded mirror as she rode. Her face was flushed, her eyes watery and blood-shot, her short, curly, reddish hair damp and messy. Why had she listened to Mandy and come here?

She must have realized he had called her for himself. When she told him over the phone that Jim might come with her, he asked, "What's wrong? You need your boyfriend for protection?"

"No," she told him. Yes, she thought, as the elevator opened on the fourteenth floor. The hallway extended to infinity in both directions. The dog knew the way. Rushing after him, she heard the high-pitched hum of the hushed, carpeted place. The dog stopped; she opened the door to 1416.

More static electricity from the wall-to-wall carpeting and the central air conditioning. The walls and floors were shades of cream and yellow, the furniture the best available in wicker and pastel. Exotic plastic plants told the familiar story of seasonal occupancy. Except for the many prints that lined the walls, the blank place won out against the poacher.

Automatically she went to the telephone. Then stopped herself. She made her way into the windowless color-coordinated kitchen that the damned dog had already found, and looked into the refrigerator to see what Herb had supplied. Greedily she took the fresh greens from the crisper. She'd start lunch for them. She did not want to think.

"You shouldn't leave the door unlocked," Mandy called from the living room, interrupting her voiceless reverie. He came to the kitchen where she was placing the lettuce she had just washed into a bowl. He held her shoulders from behind and kissed the back of her neck. "I was worried about you. Irv dozed off. Best to let him rest."

"He's dying," she said, forsaking her salad and passing by him into the living room.

"Failing's the word," Mandy said, trailing her.

She opened the sliding door and went onto the terrace where she looked down at her uncle at the pool. "All that hair."

"Makes him look ten years younger. Believe me, he's a hundred percent improved since I saw him in the hospital."

She was quiet.

"How come he didn't take the penthouse here?" Mandy asked looking up at the floors above him.

"He said he was lucky to get this."

"Some luck," said Mandy, who rented a mansion on the coast.

Back in the apartment she waved her hand at the prints on the walls and said angrily, "All these cheerful things! Why isn't there anything real? A skull he could contemplate or some worms running through fruit?"

"Like in Rome?" he asked her hoarsely.

"Don't bring up the past."

"You just did."

"No, I didn't. I was talking about death."

"You were talking about us."

"Maybe it's the same."

"What's this guy done to you? I've been through all the others, but this guy — a lawyer for a rock group? I'd rather see you with a drummer."

"Not just *one* rock group." She stopped herself. She almost bragged about Jim's success.

"I don't know him, but I don't like him."

"You are not going to know him either. Do you understand, Mandy? You're not going to join us for dinner. You're not going to treat us to a show. You're not going to drop by when you're in town."

"You gonna marry this guy?"

"We don't think in those terms."

"Really? What terms do you think in?"

"You're not going to ask personal questions!"

"What the hell are you so wound up about, sweetheart? What are you trying to say?"

"Mandy, if you really care for me, leave me alone, please."

"Don't I?" He was stunned.

"You are absurd! Our relationship is absurd!"

"You're upset."

She sat down and closed her eyes.

She is in Venice on a very hot day. An Italian has his hand between her legs. They sit at a café. "Don't you ever want to do it with someone else?" Mandy whispers, his fingers in her cunt. "You can tell me. Talk to me. Some young Italian who doesn't speak a word of English, who just takes it out and says 'Here!'" She takes out his penis, extricates it from all those buttons under the table at the café. The mosquitoes sting and buzz near her ear. He comes. He goes. Mandy moans. "Tell me it's not true," he sobs. "Don't see him again. Will you wait at the café? Will he motion to you? Will you follow? Who knows where he'll take you. These guys are all fags. Maybe he'll share you with a friend. Would you like that? Is that what you're looking for?" Hot Venice. The smell of urine. Was it the same man? Did he have a friend? She told Mandy there were two. The heat. She remembers the weight of her own sweat, of her own heart pumping, of the slow wine in her head, the formulas of English, the hard pricks, the quick coming, Mandy sobbing and screwing her.

"Say something! Talk to me! What's eating you?"

She opened her eyes. "You, Mandy, you! We can talk forever —" She stopped.

He sat down across from her. Five hundred dollars' worth of studded denim on a padded pastel chair. If only he would stay away. But he always came back to tell her he understood.

What did he understand?

"What do you mean, *me*? How do I bother you? How often do I see you? Months go by. Years."

"How adults can wait," Suzanne taunted, thinking of Beatrice's impatience. Of her own. She had wanted to burst into life. How she had wanted Larry. How quickly she had accepted Mandy. Love. He called sex love. He was incapable of love.

Unfair, Suzanne thought. Who was she to measure his emotions? She looked at the liver spots that blotched his tanned hands. She saw, like an aureole around his trim body, the quiver of feebleness that marked his inevitable decline. She didn't want him. But then she had never really wanted the man who had initiated her.

"Say something, damn you! Talk to me!"

"I have nothing to say."

"You're an obstinate bitch. You don't know the meaning of friendship."

He did. He knew it went on. In his hands it was a shackle on the past.

She sat there with her lips slightly parted, trying to tell him in silence that they were through.

"If it wasn't for this guy that's humping you —"

"How true," she said, abruptly standing. "I'm thirty-one years old and I'm still a very dependent person. If Jim didn't mind my seeing you, I'd never have had the guts to break loose! But we're not good for each other anymore, Mandy. Don't you see?"

She went out on the terrace once more and looked down on her uncle. Mandy said Irv wanted to have her near. That he needed her. Could she do anything for him? She was back in Joan Anna's farmhouse. No.

Mandy said he was failing. He was wrong. She had watched her uncle failing. He was dying now.

Mandy's arms were under her jersey. She saw his hands cupping her breasts. His thumbs irritated her nipples.

"If it's good-bye, let's do it this way," he whispered. "Not the way you do it with your friend. With him it's better, isn't it? He's young. It's not like doing it with a young man, is it?" He rubbed himself against her buttocks. He was as hard as steel.

She grasped the edge of the railing and held on.

"Come on inside. Come on in."

She stayed there, clenched on the fourteenth floor in the clear light of day with Mandy fondling her, while she looked down on her uncle's bent head.

Someone on the floor above cleared her throat. "Damn you to hell," Mandy rasped and left her there bent over the terrace.

She saw a retired couple in splendid bathing costumes walk from the building to the pool. Her uncle did not stir. His mouth was probably open, he probably drooled as he slept. The couple took the chairs across from him and turned their backs.

"What are you doing now?" Mandy said, looking up when she entered the room. She had picked up her overnight case.

"Here." She handed him the key to the apartment.

"Where are you going?"

"Home."

"Come on, Suzanne. For God's sake, sit down. I'm sorry I upset you. For God's sake, let's talk."

"You go talk to Irv! You can do him some good. I can't."

"Sweetheart," he said, and his intuition, always his sloppy angel, did not fail him. "You know what's upsetting you? You've blamed too many of your own mistakes on that poor slob sitting out there. Suddenly, he's not invulnerable, he's sick and alone and you don't know how to handle it. You used to know how to get beyond his words to his heart. Now you're afraid to try. So you blame it all on me. But I'm telling you, he wanted to see you! And I did the right thing calling you down."

Realizing with absolute conviction that he had done good, Mandy was suffused with righteousness. He lived in heaven. Time might catch up with him through loss and disease. But with a little luck — and Mandy was lucky — he would rest on his past sufferings and on his royalties. Die suddenly, oblivious to his death.

She looked at his flushed, satisfied face. They both knew he had spoken the truth. Once more he had redeemed the past between them.

She saw right through the day to the end of it. She heard the clear conversation in her ears. In her mouth she felt the weight of the words she'd use to tell him all about Jim as they masturbated one another in his suite at the Fontainebleau.

Why hadn't she let him screw her then, right then, when he was hard and eager. When just the thought of her and Jim together was enough to turn him on?

She blamed too much of her own nature on the poor slob sitting in front of her.

The truth came to her as a revelation. It made her strong. The look on her face was so soft and submissive that her action startled him. She turned her back and walked out.

She was by the elevators when she heard the scuffle. The dog barking and Mandy yelling, "Wait!" The dog got there first and circled her feet in a throe of disobedience.

Mandy arrived breathless. His face was scarlet. He grabbed her hand and pressed her uncle's key into her palm. His voice was choked with exertion and outrage. He meant to say a lot of things. But what he felt most deeply foiled him. "Don't you leave me alone with him!"

She was busy keeping the dog off the elevator. Just before the door closed, she looked in and saw surprise on Mandy's face.

⚜ ⚜ ⚜

Suzanne and Irv ate lunch together without speaking, as they did at Thanksgiving and on the Jewish holidays, only without Esther and with Beatrice's demands replaced by the dog's.

Irv reprimanded him, then snuck him bits to eat under the table.

Suzanne toyed with the Bolla Soave bottle after she poured the last glass for them.

"Shall I take your picture?" she asked, her nails clinking on the green glass.

"Here?" He looked around the dining alcove for a clue. She had never asked to photograph him before.

"Not *here*. I'm not Diane Arbus." Then she was thankful that he wouldn't understand. She saw her uncle sitting in front of the bar the closet decorator invented, next to it a lovely unreal tree. Above his ill and prosperous head, Matisse's blue bird winked.

She had told Mandy there should be skulls here to contemplate, still lifes rotten with worms. Mandy had been right. She had been thinking of images from a different time and place. Here, now, all about Irv, vacuous, fixed, and bright, was the death he could contemplate.

"Not here," she repeated. "The film I have with me works best out of doors."

She need not have bothered to cover up. Irv had gone into a trance. "I haven't got a picture of myself," he said as if it were suddenly important to have one.

He was vastly pleased. He was reassessing his importance, seeing himself at the center of things, a subject.

"So I'm going to sit for Suzanne Schwartz Bender." He said it without rancor. She was finally giving him something he really wanted.

When she spoke to him of photography, he had often shown the contemptuous disinterestedness he displayed while helping her to equip her darkroom. Perhaps for that reason, it had never occurred to her to run his face through her trays. No wonder he thought her machines were pointless.

She would have taken him to the ocean, which was not too far a walk. But that was the wine inside her, not him. He stopped by the pool.

As she arranged their seats she explained her procedure. While she was working, she felt the complete confidence of the professional. Cut off from the everyday, burrowed in her area of salvation.

She told him they would talk while they both got used to the camera that she occasionally lifted to her eye to adjust, but did not shoot.

He listened to her precise instructions in earnest. And she did something she hadn't done in years. Behind her expertise, she showed off for him.

"What should I talk about?" he asked, intrigued. As if she knew something.

"Whatever is on your mind."

"The camp. Do you want it?"

She could not answer; she was frightened by the significance of his words.

But he only meant that Ricky Lesser would like to buy in. Ricky had held the Benjamin Bender scholarship at Brandeis, and now managed the camp. He had a clean, compact body, ambition, and a wife.

"Do whatever makes things easiest for you. Let Ricky buy in. He lives for the camp. He'll do well for you."

"He cares more about himself than about the camp."

"I hope that's true."

"He's limited. He'll only go so far. Except for himself. There is nothing he won't do to help himself. You too. There is nothing you wouldn't do to find out some little scrap about yourself. As if it were important. As if it would help you out."

"When I knew very little about myself," she explained calmly, "I was hurt very badly. You made me believe I was all that mattered to you. In fact, I mattered very little."

"What do you know?" he asked, sliding past the words she never thought she'd say. "Let your analysts and your groups tell you how you feel, but don't make judgments on me."

They had made her feel the world was a fixed reality and that there were ways of setting one's mind to it and finding oneself and one's happiness. She and Jim had gone to *est* and learned how to be satisfied with what lay within their grasp.

The world had been just as fixed for Irv when he was young. But it hadn't been his. He was shrewd and had learned its ways and how to use it. But he had looked elsewhere for his home.

She thought she was entitled.

He didn't.

He bought a Ben Shahn print of Martin Luther King and took it with him to Miami on what he called his rich man's march on the South.

She went to jail for seven hours because she thought we all deserved better than Nixon and Vietnam.

He thought society was rotten except for a few men who painted or had dreams.

She thought society was repressed and guilt-ridden, but that sincere people searching for themselves could make it better.

Both were Americans, so neither envisioned a world that was radically changed.

He had listened to the lawyers at Greenspan's when they were thin and willing to fight. He committed himself to his brother, to the camp, to Larry, to nothing at all.

She saw burned-up villages, blown-up brownstones. She committed herself to finding out about herself, to living life, and, in desperation, to doing one thing well.

America was beyond their reach. America was a disenfranchised democracy. As Esther said, there was no one left to vote for, so you vote against.

The world was a fixed reality, festering, to Esther as well. Lately she spoke out, exposed her disillusionment to the air, where it had turned red as blood.

What she called her faith in people had been destroyed by Mandy Mershheimer's betrayal. But then Suzanne made contact with her again from Rome and John F. Kennedy appeared. She was never the same after his assassination, Dr. King's, Bobby's, Vietnam, the riots in Jersey City, Kent State, corruption in all high places, and women's liberation, where they burned their bras, yelled fuck you, and displayed an aggressive hostility toward men.

The news on her radio was the undulating leitmotif that underscored her daughter's abandoned recklessness and her brother-in-law's pinky rings.

She spent every minute of her free time keeping her granddaughter occupied, attempting to instill values as she played cards, Pick-Up-Sticks, records, TV. Beatrice was as good as gold when she was occupied. "Give me this, give me that —" Beatrice was being brought up by the books that said she knew what she wanted. Suzanne would look so hurt sometimes as she waited for Beatrice to make a choice. Suzanne's eyes implored, why are you holding back on me?

Esther had no illusions. Kittens were adorable, but they all grew into cats. No matter what she did for her granddaughter, the world would bloat her, make her big. Beatrice would live to see the coming cataclysm. Esther would be dead. This America wasn't hers. It wasn't the good land her own grandparents came to.

Out of a lifetime of negation, she promised herself the final gesture of contempt. She told everybody, even in front of the child, in the next election she wouldn't vote.

Suzanne heard echoes of her mother's tone in Irv's "Don't make judgments on me." She wondered if she'd have the same to say to Beatrice one day. At first she thought she had been so right about the child. It was a joy not to repeat her mother's mistakes. But it hadn't been enough. She had made her own.

She spoke to her uncle gently. "I don't judge you. I hope my daughter doesn't judge me."

"She will," he said. "She'll say you did everything wrong."

"I don't say that about you," Suzanne answered, beginning to take pictures.

"What do you say about me?"

"As little as possible."

He smiled. "You come by that honestly. Let other people talk. Listen."

"I was a good listener, wasn't I, Uncle? I was an obedient child. I listened to everybody. Everybody loved me until I began to talk."

"Talk? You shouted!" A slight smile remained on his face, as if he were secretly approving her audacity in running away years ago and in insisting since then on living her own life. He never could have run away. "You're strong-willed. When you want to, you make people listen."

"Like the way I make Mandy listen?" she asked ironically. "Have you ever tried to make Mandy listen?"

"Mandy makes you believe he can show you something. He looks over your shoulder while you're learning. Then he's on your back."

She chuckled. "Did Mandy show you anything, Uncle?"

"Short stories. Paintings. Your old friend, S. Berman Bush. Ideas. The camp. We were going to run it every summer. He'd write in the winter. Your father could have come in with us. There was room for your father too."

"Do you think of Babe often?"

"Your father?"

"Yes."

"I think of him when I look at you."

"We don't look alike."

"Around the eyes. His were blue. But big eyes like yours. And nervous too."

"I'm not nervous."

"Behind that camera you are. He was too. But he kept seeing things that weren't there. I tried to help him. Maybe you're lucky I never really could help you." He paused. "I used to wish you were a boy."

"You don't anymore?"

"What's the use? Your father's daughter, your father's son. It's all the same except the name. And you, you've kept the name."

"Thank you very much. For a moment I thought you were going to surprise me and say women were as good as men."

"They're stronger. They endure."

"They endure to see their fathers' deaths, their lovers' betrayals, their husbands' failures, and sometimes, their uncles' disinterestedness."

"Disinterestedness. Why I —"

"Bought me things. You weren't going to say you loved me, were you?"

"No. But I do." He looked away from the camera.

"Because I'm Babe's daughter."

"You are what's left."

"Am I enough?"

"Nothing is."

"Beatrice is left too."

"She's a child."

"You don't like children, do you?"

"I liked you. You were a good child. You were a wise child. I spent a lot of time with you."

"I remember."

"Do you? You don't act like you do."

"How do you act as if you remember, Uncle? Is there a way of exhibiting how it has effected what you've become?"

She looked at him through the lens. He seemed more monumental and remote. The expression on his face was one of interest at her question. She took the picture because she knew what was in her heart.

There was the man she remembered. Stripped of pretense, lost in thought.

"I wanted to ask Mandy something like that," he said.

"Why didn't you?"

"He wouldn't have been interested. I started to tell him about a terrible dream I had. He looked so bored I decided to fall asleep instead."

Sleep hadn't been Irv's *decision*, but saying it made it so. He felt hope almost like strength.

"Tell me about your dream."

"You?" He said it with something of the old tender disregard. The tone was loving, disapproving, jocular. He watched her take his picture. The camera fixed to her face. Her breasts full and soft. A ring of sweat widened on the material under her arms.

She was working. There was something unladylike about her. He remembered her old hole in the Village. He could smell her sweat.

His tone changed. "Better if I tell you to find yourself another husband and settle down."

"Oh!" She put the camera down on the table between them, stretched, and closed her eyes.

"Come on!" he said in rough repentance. "Get to work! Be moody on your own time."

"Don't give orders!" she snapped. "And if you feel free to criticize my life, I'll feel free to criticize yours. How would that suit you, Uncle?"

"It wouldn't."

"I thought not."

"You and Mandy must have discussed my life plenty."

"Only once."

"He had no right to tell you!"

"I would have found out sooner or later."

"Later would have been better!"

"Uncle Irv," she said, "you have nothing to feel guilty about." Sexually, she meant. She used the absurd words the way a psychiatrist might, to help a patient to forgive himself.

"There are certain things a man has to do in his own way. Even if he goes against the whole world. There are certain things he owes himself." He was proud and unsure.

She brought the camera to her face. "Do you ever think how strange it was that we loved the same man?"

She had shocked him without meaning to. "I don't know what you're talking about."

"I'm talking about Larry."

He looked dazed. Rather than hearing what she had said, he advanced to his habitual speculation. "I never had a chance to mourn Larry," he said decisively. "Larry slipped away from me."

"I was there. I saw you mourn him."

"What do you know? You left. You didn't care. I didn't care what you did. What Mandy did. Dirt on a coffin. But your mother. I never saw anything like Esther. After you left she was like blood gushing. Shrieking like my mother over Babe. She pulled me away from myself with her own hands. I never had a chance to mourn him. I did for her instead. She wanted me to go after you." Irv held up his hand. " 'No. Suzanne made her own bed, let her lie in it.' But I did for her. Helped her. Till I was left with a niece in Italy for her education and Larry gone."

Suzanne was astonished by this flow of words. They were new to her. But many young men had heard them through the nights.

"You were right not to come after me."

He seemed to have already forgotten what he had just said. The words were the groove in which his longings had settled. "What did you see in Mandy? How does someone like him find so many wives?"

"Mandy is interested in women the way women are interested in themselves. For a time it's a miracle. Then it's hell."

"For the women, not Mandy." Irv knew him well. "Did he put you through hell?"

"For a while. Can you imagine burning in hell forever, Uncle? They call people Christian who can think like that. Isn't it unthinkable? A shrink I know said only the insane have the ability to experience hell continually. But even they must have moments of reprieve."

"We've all lived through hell," Irv said with Limbo all around him. "Temporarily."

"Afterward it is like a dream. It can kill you while you're inside it. Then you forget and go on."

"I used to keep track of my dreams so I would remember."

"What did your dreams tell you?"

"They made me aware of certain things. One thing kept repeating. It didn't seem fair or meaningful. It still doesn't. The setting of so many of my dreams is Stegman Parkway. In my dreams I know that old place the way I can touch my own skin. The rim of grasses around the concrete backyard — each variety of weed. The taste and color of the dust on the front porch screens every spring. The little red chair with the magazines on it in the bathroom. The old gas range and the white enameled sink.

"When I walk through the rooms everything is fixed and where it was. Just where it actually was. It is only after I wake up that I realize where I've been and that it has been exactly as it was."

"Not a bad place to be," Irv interjected. "Back there with all of us."

"Oh, you're not there. None of you are. It's not Stegman Parkway while I'm asleep. It is just the setting for my dreams."

"Now shvartzers live there," said the man who had Martin Luther King on his wall.

Then he did something Suzanne had never seen him do before. He rambled. He gave her a long narration on buying that house for his mother.

She was still caught up in the mysteries of her dream. Felt the horror of being fixed in a place forever because it was where she began.

She didn't realize that it was better than being nowhere. Among a myriad of strangers on an unknown street, who is Suzanne? She thought it awful that in an indelible way she was limited and chained to her past. She had faith that she had a self. She had been taught in so many different ways that it was unique, important, her own. It did not occur to her that the rooms of Stegman Parkway were more than she was entitled to, that by clinging to her, they protected her. A shell on her back. She didn't like what was stiff and fixed and inevitable. She wanted to burst through. And she didn't like her parents' room, unrecognized, inconspicuous, without a trace of her father's corpse while she dreamed.

She wanted to be someone on her own. She was Suzanne Schwartz Bender. Given her background, her naiveté, her sex, that was something. She was a professional. Better at what she did than at what she was.

She kidded herself. She believed she would give up her photography if that renunciation would lead her to the life she so desperately wanted to live and which she could not adequately describe.

She'd never give it up — the old place on Stegman Parkway, her limitations, her work. They would hem her in. Into one of those magical places with a plaque on the door. The type of office her father could never enter.

She had Babe's tendency to self-doubt and equivocation. But she despised his fate as much as if she had been his son. She had been the daughter of only one man. She looked at her uncle through the camera as he rambled and recollected. She took a picture of him speaking of the old days in Jersey City as he sat by the pool. When he finished he seemed to forget that he had begun.

"Uncle," she called to him from behind the camera. She seemed very far away. "Tell me your dream."

He looked into the camera's eye. It had been a depressing dream. It wasn't a dream for her. He found himself at the Penny Arcade at the seashore, in Belmar, with Babe. Way before her time. It was a rainy day. Irv bought a bunch of nickels and divided them with Babe, who went away. Irv walked over to the Kinetoscope, put his eyes to the viewer and looked in. He saw the intricate mechanical workings of a vast pinball machine.

His nickels turned to years. He put the four numbers of a year into the steel slot and slid the bolt in. Many colored lights lit up, flippers flipped, the machine emitted a loud endless buzz. He tried another year. Again the garish technicolor splash of lights and signs, the frenetic movement of all the flippers. The persistent hum. Then he chose the coldest date in his hand and slid the future year in.

The lights snapped off. The machine stopped. Silence. He stared into the vast gray network of complicated mechanical parts. That was it. There was no more.

He looked at his niece with the camera on her face. He saw his mother. He saw Babe. He saw Mandy. He saw Esther. He saw her too. "I dreamed I was dead. I dreamed the universe was empty. I saw the truth. I see it now. It is nothing. It is dead. We are making something out of nothing. And what we are making is no good."

She took a picture of him with the anguish on his face. A reflex. Then she put her camera down.

The tears spilled from his eyes. She who had seen sudden death, now felt absolute horror. She was watching a living man mourn himself and she mourned too.

But the cancer growing inside him had not yet been detected. When it was discovered it would be too late. It was too late already. She knew. She intuited. But she knew nothing of the mystery of a drawn-out death. How once a death is inevitable, it takes its time, plays out an awful parody of immortality, wears down the souls of those who love one, and then, springs a surprise.

It would come to mock her — and him too — that then they thought they were near the end.

At that moment she realized Mandy would come back. He would pay his respects.

Her uncle cried like a senile man. Rigid in his chair, unable to control the flow, while water gushed from his eyes down his reddened cheeks.

"Uncle, let me take you home! Let me take you to the camp."

She saw him at Rose Lake, at the place that he had built, at the place that revolved around him, dying like a man.

She looked up and saw him framed against the looming building which still looked like an architect's mock-up, except that it was already blackening the sun. A rectangular shadow was growing, coming over him, over her. It would soon reach the pool no one used.

The setting of his death was nothing to him. At that moment she was sure he would die there among the others.

The tears stopped. He looked past her. "I am not what I started out to be," he said in rage and shame.

Her response surprised them. "I love you," she said.

The words redeemed something good in her, and in the future they served his memory.

Made in the USA
Middletown, DE
12 February 2019